AF584740

BUDDHIST MYTHS

BUDDHIST MYTHS

COSMOLOGY, TALES & LEGENDS

MARTIN J. DOUGHERTY

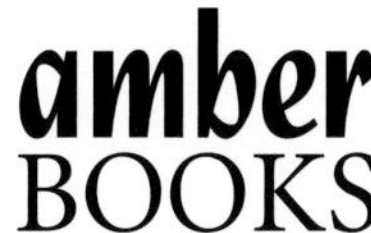

First published in 2022

Published by
Amber Books Ltd
United House
North Road
London
N7 9DP
United Kingdom
www.amberbooks.co.uk
Instagram: amberbooksltd
Pinterest: amberbooksltd
Facebook: amberbooks
Twitter: @amberbooks

ISBN: 978-1-83886-226-8

Project Editor: Michael Spilling
Designer: Keren Harragan
Picture Research: Terry Forshaw

Printed in China

CONTENTS

INTRODUCTION

Approximately 10% of the world's population practise Buddhism, a figure approaching 500 million people worldwide. It is one of the great religions of the world, though many consider it to be philosophical rather than religious in nature. Buddhism began with a single individual, Siddhartha Gautama (c.563–c.483), who gained enlightenment and began spreading his new-found knowledge.

Siddhartha Gautama is often referred to as Buddha, or the Buddha, perhaps giving the impression that there is or has been only one Buddha. This is not so; a Buddha is someone who has achieved a state of enlightenment called nirvana. There have been many Buddhas throughout history and in theory anyone can become a Buddha. It is, however, reasonable to speak of Siddhartha Gautama as 'the' Buddha as his teachings are the foundation of Buddhism. He is also known by other names,

OPPOSITE: **Here, Siddhartha Gautama sits in characteristic pose, one hand touching the earth, surrounded by historical and mythological figures, including various gods and demons.**

commonly Gautama Buddha or Shakyamuni. The first is his family name, the second a reference to his clan.

Siddhartha Gautama was born around 567 BCE, in northern India. He sought answers to his questions about why people had to suffer so much in their existence, and eventually achieved a state of enlightenment. He discovered a 'middle path' between the pleasures of his early life as a prince and the rigours of his period as a wandering ascetic, and spent the rest of his life teaching others how to tread their own path to nirvana. Gautama Buddha died around 483 BCE, after which his work was carried on by his followers.

The Spread of Buddhism

During his lifetime, the Buddha led a religious community, or Sangha, composed of monks and lay people. Monks were known

Samsara

Samsara is a Sanskrit word, translating as 'moving on' (or perhaps 'flowing on'). It refers to the endless cycle of life, death and rebirth experienced by all beings. The deeds and thoughts of a person's life, collectively referred to as Karma, dictate the nature of their next existence. This can be seen rather simplistically as a totting-up of good and bad at the end of someone's life, but it is perhaps more apt to think of it as a constant and ongoing process.

A person headed for an unpleasant next existence can always start behaving in a more positive manner, and the teachings of the Buddha explain how to go about this. However, the mortal world is imperfect and living there inevitably means at least some suffering. The only escape is to break the cycle of samsara by achieving enlightenment or nirvana. This is the ultimate goal for those who follow the teachings of Buddhism, though it can take many lifetimes to achieve.

ABOVE: All living things are trapped in samsara. Even the gods will eventually die and be reborn according to the Karma generated in life.

LEFT: Painting of Buddha preaching to an assembly of *bhiksus* (monks), in Chiang Mai, Thailand. All the monks are wearing traditional saffron-coloured robes to denote their status.

as *bhiksus* in Sanskrit, or *bhikkus* in Pali. Buddha and many of his monks wandered over a wide area, teaching wherever they went. Communities grew up, often supported by wealthy patrons who were impressed by the new religion.

After the death of Gautama Buddha, his teachings were spread by itinerant monks or revealed to those who came to visit the religious communities. There was no overall plan, just people doing what they thought best, but what would become Buddhism was sufficiently appealing that it found new adherents naturally.

In the third century BCE, the spread of Buddhism was greatly assisted by the Emperor Ashoka (c.268–c.232 BCE). Ashoka was the last of the Mauryan emperors of India. His career was marked by violence and warfare, culminating in the conquest of Kalinga in c.262 BCE. With his empire finally at peace, Ashoka devoted himself to being a fair and benevolent ruler. Perhaps he sought to give his conquests meaning beyond the obvious politico-military gains, or possibly he was weary of bloodshed and wanted a more positive existence. Whatever the reason, Ashoka became an example of the ideal ruler.

Under Ashoka's rule, all religions were tolerated and officials were charged with serving the needs of the people. This was governance on behalf of and for the benefit of the people, with

TRADITION HOLDS THAT BUDDHISM WAS INTRODUCED INTO CHINA BY THE EMPEROR MINGDI, BETWEEN 57–76 CE, IN RESPONSE TO A PROPHETIC DREAM.

projects to improve quality of life and mitigate disaster. Justice was to be fair, and Ashoka insisted that groups often ignored by lawmakers and leaders were to be protected – these included women, foreigners and the population of areas far from the main centres of governance.

Buddhism was for many years a popular religion in India, though it has since been eclipsed there. In the meantime, different interpretations of Buddha's teaching began to emerge. Mahayana Buddhism, which is today the largest of the Buddhist sects, was popular in Tibet and the north of India, and spread generally northwards. Theravada Buddhism, the oldest form, became strongly established in Sri Lanka – largely as a result of missionaries sent by Ashoka – and spread to South East Asia.

Extending into central Asia, the teachings of Buddhism encountered those of other religions, with inevitable change and competition. It remained strong in central Asia and India for several centuries but gradually waned in importance. This was in part due to the increase in importance of Hinduism and later Islam, and, by the twelfth century CE, Buddhism had all but vanished from India.

Buddhism Reaches China

Tradition holds that Buddhism was introduced into China by the Emperor Mingdi, between 57–76 CE, in response to a prophetic dream. There is evidence of Buddhist missionaries and perhaps communities as much as three centuries earlier, but the spread seems to have occurred much more quickly with official backing from the emperor. As elsewhere, major trade routes and thoroughfares were the main arteries for Buddhist teachings, with a more gradual expansion into remote areas.

Inevitably, as Buddhism spread, it came up against similar and opposing teachings. This resulted in a variety of regional flavours. In China, contact with Daoism resulted in a distortion of Buddhist principles. Chinese Buddhists seem to have preferred to believe in an immutable soul in contrast to the 'no-self' concept put forward by Gautama Buddha.

Nirvana thus became a sort of immortal condition rather than the release from the cycle of rebirth. However, the core practices of charity and self-denial were retained. Chinese Buddhist monks became associated with magic and mystical practices, and were thought to have arcane knowledge of many subjects. As a result, they were sought out or offered patronage in return for their wisdom, becoming part of the political and even military landscape.

Under the Sui dynasty of 581–618 CE, Buddhism was the state religion. It continued to thrive in the years that followed, but fell into disfavour in the 800s CE. Under Emperor Wuzong, Buddhists were systematically persecuted in the year 845 CE, with hundreds of holy places destroyed.

Thereafter, Chinese Buddhism was diminished but remained a popular religion in much of China, existing alongside Daoism and Confucianism. The most prevalent schools of Buddhism were the Chan school, which emphasized meditation and is better known as Zen Buddhism, and the Pure Land school.

ABOVE: The Sanguan Dadi are the Three Great Officials of Daoism who oversee the realms of earth, water and sky. Like Buddhism, Daoism is driven by philosophy rather than obedient worship of gods.

From China, Buddhism spread southwards into Korea, beginning in the fourth century CE, and south-eastwards into what is now Cambodia, Laos and Vietnam. From Korea, it reached Japan in the sixth century CE. Adoption was patchy and caused conflict with those who believed the new religion was a threat or insult to their existing gods. By the mid-700s, Buddhism was the official state religion in Japan, although there were strong influences from local religions such as Shinto, which created a new set of Buddhist schools.

By the early 1600s, Buddhism was a tool of governance used by the Tokugawa shogunate. Temples were administrative centres and enthusiasm was encouraged as a way of countering the work of Christian missionaries who had begun to arrive

ABOVE: **Tokugawa Ieyasu founded the shogunate in Japan, and is considered by some to have possessed a divine spirit. Buddhism was an important social and administrative tool in Japan until the end of the shogunate.**

Political change, in the form of the Meiji Restoration in the mid–late 1800s caused Buddhism to fall into disfavour due to associations with the shogunate. It remained a part of the religious landscape in Japan, albeit in diminished form.

The northward spread into Tibet and beyond is traditionally said to have begun in the early 600s. After flourishing for a while, it was suppressed for nearly two hundred years, but then rapidly developed into the region's dominant religion and cultural force. Tibetan Buddhism continued to spread northwards into Mongolia. Even leaders of the great (and extremely violent) Mongol Empire were impressed; Kublai Khan (1216–94), the fifth Mongol Emperor, actively supported Tibetan Buddhism.

Overlaps and Influences

The spread of Buddhism was not simple or clear-cut. There is evidence of Buddhist groups in some areas much earlier than the official 'arrival date' recorded by history, and considerable overlap between regions. For example, the Mongol Empire conquered China and controlled it from 1279 –1368. Thus, the Tibetan-flavoured Buddhism that had taken hold in Mongolia was supported in China for a time.

Existing local religions affected which Buddhist beliefs were more likely to take hold, making the Theravada or Mahayana schools preferable or causing a mingling of local and Buddhist practices. In some cases, these modified versions of Buddhism then encountered further local religions as they expanded, creating ever greater variety around the same central concepts.

One of the religions encountered was Christianity. There is some evidence that Buddhist travellers might have been abroad in the Middle East during the early development of Christianity, and that there may have been some cultural exchange. However, there was no significant spread of Buddhism into the Western world until the modern era.

Stupas

Stupas are holy sites taking the form of a free-standing monument that may or may not be contained within a building. They were originally built to house holy relics from the life of the Buddha, though later it became common to place religious texts inside. Designs vary, largely as a result of regional differences, but the original stupas were based on burial mounds predating the rise of Buddhism. In China, Japan and Korea, stupas often take the form of a pagoda, and the term 'pagoda' is used apparently interchangeably in Buddhist writings.

BELOW: The Great Stupa at Sanchi in Madhya Pradesh is one of the oldest Buddhist structures in India.

The Chinese occupation of Tibet caused some religious figures to relocate to the West and others to move to areas where they were more likely to encounter Westerners.

In the meantime, colonial and economic activity in the Far East brought Buddhism to the attention of at least some Westerners. Long regarded as a curiosity or a subject for intellectuals, Buddhism became attractive to a wider audience during the troubled years of the mid-twentieth century. Perhaps seeking new answers in the frightening Cold War world, increasing numbers of Westerners began turning to Buddhism. For some, it was an affectation or the equivalent of a fashion accessory, but not for everyone, and now Buddhism has finally gained a solid foothold in the West.

Languages of Buddhism

The languages of northern India evolved from the Proto-Indo-European language, which developed into several linguistic groups over time. One such was the Indo-Iranian language group, which further evolved into what are known as the Indo-Aryan languages. Modern (or New) forms of these languages are spoken in Pakistan, through to Bangladesh and Sri Lanka. Linguists have identified more ancient forms categorized as Middle and Old Indo-Aryan languages.

BELOW: According to Mongolian legend, the double-headed Buddha statue represents how Buddha divided a sculptor's work so that two poor men who could only afford a statue between them could each have one.

Sanskrit is one of the Old Indo-Aryan languages, in which the Vedas were written around 1500–1200 BCE. The Vedas are epic poems containing a vast array of knowledge, which forms the basis of the Vedic religion. This was the beginning of what is today called Hinduism. Buddha chose not to use Sanskrit in his teachings as it required education, instead speaking in the common dialects, which would be easily understood by ordinary people.

The primary language of Buddha's early teachings was Pali, a Middle Indo-Aryan language that was related to but not descended directly from Sanskrit. Since much of Buddha's teaching was first recorded in Pali, it became the standard canonical language of Buddhism. Pali fell out of common use in India during the fourteenth century but was retained elsewhere for the next four centuries.

Variants of Buddhism

There are three main Buddhist sects in the modern world, known as Theravada, Mahayana and Vajrayana. Theravada Buddhism, translating loosely as 'way of the elders', is mainly found in south-eastern Asia, from Sri Lanka to Cambodia and Thailand. It dates back to the earliest Buddhist communities and retains their traditions. Theravada Buddhism is primarily concerned with the liberation of the individual from the sufferings of existence. Its texts are in Pali, and adherents are required to join a monastic community.

Mahayana Buddhism, or the 'great way' is more concerned with helping others than the individual. Within the general grouping of Mahayana Buddhism are several sub-groups, including Tibetan Buddhism, Zen Buddhism and Pure Land Buddhism. The latter is attractive to people who struggle to follow the path required to reach enlightenment. By placing faith in Amitabha Buddha, the individual hopes to be reborn in the 'pure land', where it is much easier and simpler to work towards enlightenment. It is common in Japan and China. Mahayana Buddhism is also common in Korea, Mongolia and Tibet.

Where Theravada Buddhism centres on a personal journey to enlightenment as part of a monastic order, Mahayana Buddhism puts aside the self in favour of achieving perfection as a Bodhisattva; a being who has achieved enlightenment for the sake of everyone.

ABOVE: Vairocana is considered by some Buddhists to be the first of the Dhyani (or Transcendent) Buddhas. The position of his hands denotes his connection with the zenith of the cosmos.

Vajrayana, or the 'Diamond School' of Buddhism, was prevalent in Tibet until the events of the twentieth century forced a relocation. It is attractive to a wide range of people, including those whose lives do not permit the sort of focus required in other forms of Buddhism. Vajrayana Buddhism has spread worldwide, including into Western nations, notwithstanding the large cultural differences encountered.

Despite being recognized as one of the world's great religions, Buddhism differs from most of the others. There is no single 'true and correct Buddhism', though many would say they think they have found one, and Buddhism takes a very different view of deities compared to most religions. A great many gods are acknowledged and respected, but they are considered to be powerful beings within the same frame of reference as humans and animals rather than the creators and rulers of the cosmos.

The gods, like everyone else, are bound by the cycle of samsara. They are born and they die. A person might be reincarnated as a god and then a human again, in a cycle of endless lives, until they achieve enlightenment and break out of the cycle of samsara. This requires achieving the state known as nirvana by following the principles laid down by the Buddha.

1

CONCEPTS AND COSMOLOGY

The oldest Buddhist writings describe the cosmos in terms of a mortal realm with 'heavens' above and 'hells' below, but this model is by no means universal. Other Asian religions have clearly influenced Buddhist thinking, creating numerous visions of the cosmos. However, cosmology may be less important in Buddhism than in other religions since the self is central.

At the time Gautama Buddha became enlightened, the dominant religion in India was Hinduism, whose original teachings were contained in the Vedas. These defined the cosmos and the place of gods, humans and other creatures within it. Hinduism did not present a clear-cut explanation of exactly how the universe came to be, and encouraged its adherents to seek their own answers. It is likely that Gautama Buddha grew up with this universal model and mindset, and that his journey to enlightenment was guided by them.

OPPOSITE: A depiction of Buddhist heavens, one above the other, from the Tibetan tradition. Buddhism does not consider attaining heaven an end goal, though some heavens are a stepping stone to enlightenment.

Both Buddhism and Hinduism view the universe as cyclical, but one critical difference is that while Hinduism requires the work of gods to bring about changes in the cosmos, Buddhism holds that the process is natural and everything is interconnected. Indeed, it is the interactions of beings within the cosmos with it and each other that cause the universe itself to change in particular ways.

BELOW: Siddhartha Gautama was born into a noble family and lived his early life as a prince. This was the culmination of many lifetimes, during which he accrued virtue and wisdom, until he was finally ready to begin his ultimate progress to enlightenment.

The constant cycle of rebirth means that humans are forced to endure the sufferings of existence over and over again, and it is the nature of people that causes the world to be shaped the way it is. Buddha told a story of how at the beginning of a new cycle of creation, everyone was a formless and happy creature floating about in the proto-universe. As solid objects began to appear, the beings investigated them and were at first pleased. However, the cravings at the core of every being caused them to desire to possess what was freely available, and this resulted in the beings becoming diminished, eventually morphing into the familiar form of humanity, with all its defects, shortcomings and earthly desires. This, in turn, caused the world to degenerate and the suffering of humans to increase.

By this logic, selfish and antisocial behaviour does not merely affect those nearby; it damages the whole cosmos. On the other hand, a world filled with enlightened people or those diligently working towards enlightenment would be a significantly nicer place.

Fundamentals of Buddhism

Buddhism has developed over the centuries, with variants appearing in different regions. At the heart of all are the fundamental principles realized by Buddha. These begin with the Four Noble Truths.

Gods and Other Powerful Beings

Buddhism recognizes the existence of several powerful beings. The Devas are gods, but they are not all-powerful. Indeed, the Devas, like all other beings, are trapped in the cycle of death and rebirth. Someone reincarnated as a Deva might live an incredibly long life by human standards and have experiences beyond the mortal realm, but ultimately they are part of the universe and subject to its cycles of rebirth.

The Asuras are sometimes referred to as 'demons' or 'titans'. They are god-like beings who are generally at odds with the Devas. Asuras are not intrinsically evil or ill-intentioned but they cause a great deal of trouble in the cosmos. Other, lesser, supernatural beings also exist but all of them are subject to the same cycles as humans.

BELOW: A bas-relief of Devas battling Asuras, from the temple of Angor Wat, Cambodia. Conflict between these groups arose from the coarse behaviour of the Asuras.

The first of the Truths is known as *dukkha* in Pali, or *duhkha* in Sanskrit. Suffering or sorrow is a consequence of existence, due to many kinds of pain. This can be directly caused, such as the pain accompanying sickness or old age, but it can also stem from the passing of a moment of pleasure or the inevitability that pain will return at some point.

The second of the Truths is *samudaya*, an understanding known as the Three Poisons, Three Fires or Three Roots of Evil.

These are greed or a desire for pleasure; an unfulfilled ambition or delusion; and hatred. Thus a physical injury causes a deeper type of suffering in the form of the unfulfilled desire for the pain to stop.

The third Truth is that there is a way to cease suffering, and is known as *nirodha*. Since all things are impermanent, pleasure or the absence of pain will not last forever. By letting go of attachment to the present situation or the expectation of pleasure, it is possible to negate the suffering caused by an imperfect, impermanent existence. This state is known as nirvana. It is not a heaven or otherworldly realm but a state of being. Having turned away from the cravings that make existence unpleasant, an enlightened person is freed from the suffering they cause.

BELOW: The quintessential image of the Buddha derives from the art of the Gupta Period, 400–600 CE. These carvings include depictions of the Four Essential Truths of the Eightfold Path.

The fourth Truth is a guide to what a person can do to reach nirvana. The process is neither easy nor simple, and consists of eight areas of endeavour making up the Eightfold Path. This is not a set of 'steps to enlightenment' but a guide to all the things a person must do in their life – all at the same time – in order to achieve the goal of nirvana. Buddha stated that the Eightfold Path is a tool or a vehicle, and is no longer needed when nirvana is achieved.

Samma ditthi, or 'right understanding' is the acceptance of Buddhist teachings. This is not blind faith; Buddha explicitly told his followers that they were to ponder what he taught them and draw their own conclusions. It is not

possible to be led to enlightenment by carefully performing rituals or following instructions; Buddhists must find their own way there, with the Eightfold Path as a helpful map.

Samma sankappa, or 'right intention' is the endeavour to develop the right outlook and attitudes. Few people can radically change their worldview in an instant, at least not without descending into self-delusion. It is necessary to work constantly towards a true and real alignment with the correct principles.

Samma vaca, or 'right speech', refers to honesty and integrity when dealing with others. A Buddhist is expected to speak the truth and not to say hurtful things, especially if they are untrue. Petty gossip or denigrating someone's achievements leads to suffering, not enlightenment.

Samma kammanta, or 'right action', refers to living in peace and trying to get along with others. Actions that harm others or society as a whole, such as thievery and violence, cannot lead to enlightenment. It is acceptable to enjoy life and to indulge in worldly pleasures, but only to a moderate degree.

Samma ajiva, or 'right livelihood' refers to making a living in an honest manner that does not harm others – directly or

ABOVE: The Eightfold Path is often depicted as the spokes of a wheel, as shown here. It is not a simple, straight road to be trodden once but a long cycle of correct behaviour, thought and meditation that eventually leads to enlightenment.

Karma

The concept of Karma existed in Indian religion in Gautama Buddha's time and was adopted into his philosophy. Essentially, a person accumulates 'moral energy' as a result of their actions, good and bad, and carries it over from one life to the next. The only way to break out of the cycle of endless rebirth (and therefore continued suffering) is to achieve enlightenment and cast off the shackles of Karma.

Karma is widely misunderstood in the Western world, and it is useful to draw a distinction between Karma in a religious context and karma (without capitalization) as a distorted pop-culture concept. In popular Western conception, people see someone who has done a bad deed suffer misfortune and refer to it as 'instant karma', or witness the downfall of an unpleasant person and ascribe it to accumulated 'bad karma'. While there may be some cause and effect at play in these circumstances, this is not Karma. Karma is much more long term, causing a bad person to suffer over endless lifetimes until they finally change their behaviour and outlook and start working towards enlightenment.

In short, it is karma when someone runs a red light in front of a police car and gets a ticket to the amusement of onlookers, and Karma if they drive so inconsiderately that they are reborn as a slug.

OPPOSITE: A depiction of the Arhat (someone who has achieved a state of nirvana) Kalika, one of eighteen original followers of Buddha who achieved enlightenment and were tasked with protecting Buddhism until the arrival of the next Buddha.

otherwise. This precludes occupations connected with supplying harmful substances, and also unethical practices such as unfairly benefiting from or taking credit for someone else's work.

Samma vayama, or 'right effort', refers to a positive outlook on the world and a refusal to dwell on the negative, accompanied by positive deeds whenever they are possible.

Samma sati, or 'right mindfulness', refers to paying attention to one's own body and mind. Without self-awareness of negative states or self-delusion, it is not possible to progress towards a state of enlightenment.

Samma samadhi, or 'right concentration', refers to developing the perception and habitual self-awareness necessary for a good state of mindfulness.

The Eightfold Path requires the person to possess the wisdom to want to follow it, the mental discipline and focus to be able to follow it, and the ability to differentiate between ethical behaviour and self-interest or the short-sighted desire to satisfy cravings. These traits are developed over time and represent a development of the person rather than something imposed from outside by religious dogma.

AN INDIVIDUAL WHO HAS NOT ACHIEVED NIRVANA IS TRAPPED IN AN ENDLESS CYCLE OF REBIRTH, KNOWN AS SAMSARA, WHICH MEANS THAT THE SUFFERING INHERENT IN EXISTENCE LASTS FOREVER.

Most religions are quite clear on the questions of whether people have souls and the nature of the soul, but Buddhism differs on this point. Indeed, whereas Hinduism posits the existence of a permanent *atman*, or 'self', Buddhism considers the permanent self to be an illusion. A person is how they are at this moment, and only in this moment. Their experiences and interactions with the world cause a constant change in the person such that there is no immutable soul, only a product of an endless and ongoing set of experiences.

The experience of existence is described in terms of interactions and perceptions. An individual who has not achieved nirvana is trapped in an endless cycle of rebirth, known as samsara, which means that the suffering inherent in existence lasts forever. The only way to break the cycle is to achieve nirvana, at which point the enlightened being can live out their remaining years in peace and contentment before leaving the cycle of rebirth. This is not the same concept as 'ascending to heaven'; it is more complex and is not clearly explained in the teachings of Buddha.

A person's experience of the world is defined by five *skandhas*, or groupings. *Rupa* is material existence, in the sense of what can be perceived about an object rather than just a neat definition of its type. Physical characteristics include states of matter – fluid, solid, hot, moving or static – along with numerous secondary characteristics, such as body, touch, sound, odour and taste. The other four *skandhas* are *vedana* (sensations or feelings), *samjna* (perception and discernment of characteristics), *samskara* (mental or psychological impressions) and *vijnana* (consciousness by way of the physical senses or the mind).

The Law of Twelve Causes

According to the teachings of the Buddha, there are twelve factors that cause constant change in the universe and the people who inhabit it. This is known as the Law of Twelve Causes or the Doctrine of the Twelve-Link Chain of Dependent Origination. The law applies to physical and mental changes in a person as well as the wider universe, but is particularly important to the development of people.

The first of the Twelve Causes is Ignorance. This has more than one meaning. The very fact that a person is born as a human means they are ignorant – in the sense that they did not achieve enlightenment – in previous lives. It is also true that before conception, a person does not exist and therefore cannot perceive or experience anything. In this sense, ignorance is total.

The second stage is Action. In the case of humans, this means conception, after which consciousness develops. That term can be misleading, as a foetus in the womb is not conscious in the sense that an adult human would be. However, the foetus is capable of having experiences and is therefore a part of the world.

The fourth link is Name and Form. This refers to the development of a person with a distinct physical form and an identity. The development of this person continues with the Six Entrances, which refers to their five senses and mental ability to make use of the information they provide. The Six Entrances permit the next stage, Contact, to take place. This is meaningful interaction with the wider universe, and is followed by Sensation. Sensation arises out of processing the information provided by the Six Entrances and developing an understanding of the surrounding universe as well as opinions – likes and dislikes – about some of its elements.

Sensation naturally leads to Desire (or Craving), in the sense of forming attachments and desiring to avoid unpleasant circumstances, and further develops into Clinging (or Grasping). At this point, the developing person enters the stage called

Three Jewels

The Triratna, or 'three jewels', that comfort Buddhists are the Buddha, the Sangha – the community of fellow believers – and Dharma. Dharma is the universal truth discovered by the Buddha. The term is also used in the plural to describe the various elements of the universe and how they interrelate.

ABOVE: A pendant dating from 185–172 BCE representing the Triratna, or the 'three jewels' of Buddhism. These are the Buddha, the Dharma and the monastic community.

Existence (or Becoming), characterized by all manner of cravings and attachments and therefore beset by suffering. Living this life is referred to as Birth, which is followed by Old Age and Death.

The Complex Cosmos

The cosmos, as described in Buddhist texts, is complex and is considered to have both spatial and temporal elements. Many aspects of this cosmology are based on the beliefs prevalent in India at the time of Buddha's life, and are very similar to those of Hinduism. The universe consists of a mortal realm, with 'heavens' above it and 'hells' below.

BELOW: Mandalas of this sort serve as a map, helping mortals visualize the cosmos and the interrelation of its elements. These Tibetan mandalas depict the five Transcendent Buddhas.

The universe comes into being at the start of a cycle, and each of the worlds within it is created when the first being is born there. At the beginning the world, everything in it is bright and new, but over time, degeneration inevitably occurs. The poor Karma of the people within a world will drag it down until eventually the universe must be destroyed and remade. This is a natural process, with no requirement for godly intervention, as is seen in other religions.

Time has different meanings and varying relevance in Buddhism. Progress towards nirvana can take many lifetimes, and those may be of vastly different lengths. It is possible both to be reborn as a very long-lived god-like being or to lead a short and unfortunate existence before being reborn in another set of circumstances altogether.

The longest unit of time is the *maha-kalpa*, translating as 'great aeon'. This is the time required for a complete cycle of creation, stability, destruction and nothingness before the next great aeon begins. Each of these four stages is one *asankya-kalpa*, or 'aeon', long. Each *asankya-kalpa* is subdivided into twenty *antah-kalpas*, or 'small *kalpas*'. The term '*kalpa*' is also used more loosely to refer to an extremely long period of time, with the possibility that some *kalpas* might be much longer than others.

TIME HAS DIFFERENT MEANINGS AND VARYING RELEVANCE IN BUDDHISM. PROGRESS TOWARDS NIRVANA CAN TAKE MANY LIFETIMES, AND THOSE MAY BE OF VASTLY DIFFERENT LENGTHS.

Buddha gave an impression of the periods involved by way of an analogy. If someone were to gently wipe a mountain-sized boulder with a silk cloth once a century, the rock would be completely worn away before the end of the *kalpa*. Comparisons might be drawn to geological time or the lifespans of stars, but it is still difficult to conceptualize such a great span of years. That difficulty is sufficient for most purposes – a *kalpa* is an unimaginably long period of time.

Buddhist texts also refer to the *ksana*. In modern terms this is defined as one seventy-fifth of a second, but in context, *ksana* can be thought of as 'an instant': a tiny duration too short to be consciously observed. Precise measurements of time are generally unnecessary and may well be illusory. However, relative time is important in some ways.

Some Buddhist texts refer to three periods of time relevant to the Dharma that are revealed by the Buddha. The Former Day of the Law (or Age of True Dharma) refers to the thousand years after the death of Buddha. During this time, his teachings were passed on correctly. The Middle Day of the Law (or Age of the Semblance of the Law) is said to last a thousand years, or five hundred years, depending on the source. During this time, the teachings of the Buddha are passed on, but imperfectly and in a manner emphasizing empty ritual rather than real understanding. While more people know about the Buddha's teachings in this period, fewer reach enlightenment.

The third period is ten thousand years long and is known as the Latter Day of the Law (or Age of the Decadent Law). During this time, the teachings of Buddha have become garbled, and monks are more inclined to squabble over interpretations or petty disputes than to perform useful work. The importance of these time periods varies from one source to another.

The Mortal World

The mortal world is a disc centring upon Mount Meru in the Himalayas, with seven concentric mountain ranges and finally a wall of iron known as Cakravala surrounding the whole world. The universe revolves around the central mountain. Day and night are caused by the sun passing behind Mount Meru, which is 80,000 yojanas high – some sources say 84,000 – and extends the same distance below the disc. A yojana varies between sources, with some placing the summit of Mount Meru over a million kilometres (621,370 miles) above the plane of the surface world.

BELOW: This mandala depicting Mount Meru at the centre of the cosmos comes from China but follows the traditions of Indian mythology, which were prevalent when Buddhism first arose.

According to tradition inherited from the Indian religion of the time, Mount Meru is vastly wider at its summit and lowest point, tapering down to meet the surface world then widening again below. The mountain has five peaks, and its summit intersects the lowest of the higher 'worlds'. The world inhabited by mortals surrounds the mountain and is mostly made up of golden earth. Below this is a layer of water, then a layer of air and finally a layer of void, or space.

Apart from the Cakravala, which is composed of iron, the seven concentric mountain ranges are made of the same earth as the land below. They are named Meru, Yugandhara, Isadhara, Khadirika, Sudarsana, Asvarkana, Vinatka and Nimindhara. Each range is half the height of the last, and extends as far below the surface in the same manner as Mount Meru.

Between the mountain ranges are oceans, with four major land masses located in the outermost of them – between Nimindhara and Cakravala. The northern land mass is named Uttarakuru, the southern Jambudvipa. In the east is Purvavideha, while Aparagodaniya is in the west. On three of these land masses, human lifespan is long and remains so throughout the cycles of creation and destruction. This is not the case on Jambudvipa.

BELOW: A 'cosmic map' depicting the layout of the cosmos in the traditional Indian mythological manner. The same general view of the cosmos is common to Hinduism, Jainism and Buddhism.

Uttarakuru is at times described as a place in the mortal world; on other occasions it is said to be a mythical land. It is square, 2,000 yojanas on each side and populated by wealthy people who live a thousand years. Having everything they need readily available, the people of Uttarakuru are not beset by greed.

Aparagodaniya is circular, and is inhabited by extremely tall humans who live for five hundred years – half as long as the people of Uttarakuru. They do not build houses but are content to sleep on the ground.

The people of Purvavideha, which is semicircular, are about twice as tall as normal humans and live for two hundred and fifty years.

Although these continents are pleasant places in which to live, spiritual development towards enlightenment cannot occur there. Only on Jambudvipa is this possible, but it comes at a price.

At the beginning of a new cycle, when the world is new and wonderful, humans on Jambudvipa live so long that their spans cannot be reckoned. As the world inevitably degenerates, people live shorter lives. At the very end, when the world is due to be destroyed and remade, a lifetime is only ten years. Given the horrific state of the world and the constant misery of existing in it by that point, a decade is probably quite enough.

ABOVE: Three of the four *dvipas* – islands, or continents – that surround Mount Meru are magical lands where human lifespans are extremely long. Only in Jambudvipa is it possible to achieve enlightenment. Perhaps not coincidentally, life in Jambudvipa can be quite unpleasant.

Although Jambudvipa seems to be the worst option for a place to live, at least most of the time, it is essential to the cosmos in a way the other lands are not. Only in Jambudvipa can a Buddha appear, and then only as the world is becoming unpleasant. Beings can have long and joyful lives elsewhere, but only in Jambudvipa can they become enlightened and finally escape the cycle of rebirth. Although it is not the geographical centre of the cosmos, Jambudvipa is something of a spiritual axis. Above it are the heavens and below are the hells.

Six Realms

Sources vary on exactly how many realms make up the universe and how they are subdivided. Some early sources cite five realms, later expanded to six. These are the main components of the cosmos but are not necessarily physical locations. There is a metaphysical element to these worlds, in the sense that someone can be 'in the realm of the hungry ghosts' in terms of their mindset and situation, even if they are physically occupying a small part of the normal mortal realm.

Similarly, some of the terminology used can be confusing due to there being a different meaning in other religions. Although the terms 'heaven' and 'hell' are widely used, the context of these words is different from that found in most other faiths. A being might be reborn in a heaven or a hell and live out a life there, but these places are imperfect and impermanent like everything else. Eventually, the cycle of death and rebirth will take its course and the individual may be reborn elsewhere. A life spent in a heaven might be very pleasant but the only way to progress towards enlightenment is to live in the mortal world.

Deva-gati is home to the Devas, or gods. They are sometimes referred to as 'the thirty-three' as some early Vedic lore cites that number of deities. However, other sources include additional gods that increase the total. The term is now a figure of speech referring to an unspecified number of gods. The Devas are part of the cycle of decay and rebirth like all other beings in the cosmos, but on a much longer time scale. When they finally

BELOW: Asuras are not necessarily inimical to humans, and can be good friends to them. However, they are jealous and prideful, and prone to anger, which can lead to them lashing out against people or other Asuras.

ABOVE: Images of supernatural places are common adornments for Buddhist stupas. This one depicts Devi-Gati, home of the gods.

die, Devas will be reborn elsewhere in the cosmos. They cannot achieve enlightenment in Deva-gati, making an existence there a pleasant interlude or even a task to be accomplished rather than an end goal. Rebirth into this realm results from wholesome actions and the development of wisdom.

Manusa-gati is the human realm, with all the inherent contradictions and complexities that beset our daily lives. This is the only realm from which it is possible to achieve enlightenment, possibly because it is the most confusing and difficult. The other realms are rather one-dimensional, which limits the choices a person can make. It may be that enlightenment is only possible to those who have weathered the full complexity of mortal life. Rebirth into Manusa-gati represents a middle path through the cosmos, threading between the pleasures of heaven and the torments of hell.

Asura-gati is the home of the Asuras. They are powerful but rather antisocial, embodying the life choices and mindset that result in rebirth in Asura-gati. Those who are resentful, jealous and hateful may spend a lifetime in Asura-gati before returning to the cycle in another realm. Like Deva-gati, this is a dead end for those who desire enlightenment. The life of an Asura is characterized by constant envy of one another and desire to stand above them. This makes existence as one less pleasant than being a Deva, though there is some rather toxic satisfaction to be gained by exercising power and getting one up on a rival.

Preta-gati is the realm of hungry ghosts. Rebirth as a Preta befalls those who hunger for or crave too much. This could be a literal greed for food, but more commonly it reflects an excessive or even obsessive desire for something that may not be physical. An unhealthy craving for money, power, knowledge or even enlightenment can lead to a period spent in Preta-gati.

Tiryagyoni-gati is the 'realm of animals', though this does not necessarily mean being reborn as an animal. Wilful ignorance, prejudice and general stupidity can result in an individual living in an animal state – essentially unaware of the wider world and content with a very basic existence. Progress towards enlightenment is not possible for those who exist at this primitive level. Rebirth into this realm results from wilful ignorance and lack of virtue, but there is some comfort for those who were generous to holy people despite being otherwise unwholesome.

LEFT: This sculpture at Mount Baoding in China depicts Naraka-gati, a hell realm reserved for the worst criminals and people who are argumentative for no good reason.

OPPOSITE: The Buddha spent some time in the Trāyastriṃa heaven, teaching the Dharma to his deceased mother, before returning to earth to continue his work there. This depiction of his descent to earth comes from Thailand.

They return as attractive animals such as brightly coloured birds, whereas those who completely lack virtue may be reincarnated as worms, slugs and similarly unappealing creatures.

Naraka-gati is the 'hell realm' and is associated with violence and anger. As with the other realms, rebirth into Naraka-gati results in an existence spent embodying the poor behaviour and negative emotions that caused the individual to be there in the first place. Naraka-gati is thus an unpleasant place, where conflict or violence can break out on the merest pretext. Rebirth here is reserved for the worst of people – those who murder their parents, create division in a religious community or who are generally annoying. Rebirth in hell is not eternal punishment but a rather extreme form of rehabilitation. When an individual has suffered enough to remove their bad Karma, they are reborn somewhere else.

The Sensuous Worlds

The realms of the cosmos are subdivided, creating a total of thirty-one worlds when the mortal realm is included. These worlds are located on four planes, of which the lowest contains the four hells. These correspond to the realms of the Asuras, Pretas, Animals and the Hell Realm. It is notable that five of the six realms – four hells and one mortal plane – are distinct single worlds whereas the 'heavens' are vastly more complex and consist of twenty-six distinct worlds.

Above the hells are the Sensuous Worlds, or Kama-Loka. In these worlds, everything – good and bad – is experienced through the Six Entrances. All five senses and the mind are at play, and the pleasures of the heavens are sensory. The lowest of these is the human realm, with various heavens above. The first of these is Catummaharajika Deva, home to the Four Heavenly Kings. Each is associated with a cardinal direction of the compass and commands other supernatural creatures. Their mission is to defend the Dharma and to protect the Buddha. The Four Heavenly Kings serve Sakra, a Deva who dwells in the next world above. Catummaharajika Deva is said to be located on the slopes of Mount Meru.

Trāyastriṃa Deva, or The World of the Thirty-three Gods, is home to the Hindu deities recognized by Buddhism. They are

powerful and influential but are not worshipped in the same way as gods in other religions might be.

Trāyastriṃa is located atop Mount Meru, and is the highest world that has a physical connection to the mortal world. One consequence of this is that the imperfections of the mortal world can affect the Devas, trapping them in the same cycle of decay and rebirth as the rest of the cosmos. Trāyastriṃa Deva is ruled by the Deva Sakra, who correlates to the Hindu god Indra. He also directs the Four Heavenly Kings.

BELOW: Mara attempted to interfere with Buddha's mediation by sending an army of demons. Despite their best efforts, they could not harm him, nor even get him to acknowledge their presence.

Above Trāyastriṃa lies the world of the Yama Devas, where all the senses are delighted. Those who dwell in this world have risen above their conflict with the Asuras. Next above is Tusita Deva, the Joyful Land or Land of Contented Devas. In addition to Devas, Tusita Deva is where Buddhas reside before being born on earth. The Bodhisattva Natha currently exists in Tusita Deva, awaiting the time to be reborn on earth as the next Buddha.

The next world above is Nimmanarati Deva, home to Devas who delight in creation. These beings can conjure anything into existence by thought alone. The highest of the Kama-Loka worlds is Paranimmita Deva, or Parinirmita-Vasavartin Deva. It is home to Devas who do not create but enjoy the creations of those seeking their favour. The ruler of this world is Vasvartin, who has the best of everything. It is also home to Mara, a powerful and complex figure. Mara is sometimes conflated with Vasvartin, but other sources say they are separate beings.

Mara is most definitely an opponent of the Buddha, and is sometimes described as 'the evil one'. However, this is more due to conflicting agendas than enmity for its own sake. Mara has dominion over all beings who are subject to samsara – those who are within the cycle of Karma and rebirth. Anyone who achieves nirvana escapes this cycle and is beyond the control of Mara. Naturally, this results in opposition to the work of the Buddhas.

Mara attained his lofty position as a result of noble deeds in past lives and is not inimical as such to the people of the mortal realm. Arguably, by denying them enlightenment, he does prolong their suffering, but this is a by-product of his agenda rather than his main aim, and he does not go abroad in the world spreading misery on his own account. Indeed, there are tales in which Mara is convinced to stop impeding the move towards enlightenment, and even to promise that someday he will work towards being a Buddha. This represents perhaps the greatest of all victories, which would be to persuade Mara to work towards freeing mortals from his own dominion.

Mara made several efforts to prevent the enlightenment of Guatama Buddha. First, he tried to prevent the Buddha from leaving his palace to begin seeking enlightenment. When this failed, Mara sent an army of monsters to disturb Buddha as he meditated under the Bodhi tree. When the monsters proved unable to harm or even disturb the Buddha, Mara tried a different approach. He proclaimed his own merit, which was confirmed by his hordes of followers. However, Buddha's worthiness was confirmed by the earth goddess herself.

In some sources, Mara also attempted to distract Buddha by sending his three daughters to seduce him. Naturally, the Buddha was immune to their charms. His final trick was to try to prevent Buddha from spreading his wisdom by passing into parinirvana straight away. Had he done this, Buddha would have left the mortal world immediately and anyone else seeking

BELOW: Mara also attempted to prevent Buddha from making his Great Departure – the moment of renunciation of the mundane world – and later tried temptation to lure him aside from the path. Buddha's victories over these efforts were quiet ones, but profound.

enlightenment would have had to start from the very beginning.

Mara's interference did not end with challenging the Buddha. At various times, he has tried to deceive or intimidate followers of Buddhism with false teachings, misleading words or outright threats. Mara is blamed for almost any interference or setback encountered by a Buddhist individual or community. He and his daughters have therefore become metaphors for the cravings, desires and other inappropriate characteristics that hold mortals back from enlightenment.

FOUR JHANAS

The four *jhanas* are stages of meditation. The first is attained by putting aside the external world in deep meditation, focusing on a sense of joy and ease. The second stage concentrates on this sense, putting aside questions and reasoning. The third stage allows joy to pass away, leaving only a sense of ease. The fourth stage is attained when even this state of ease is gone, leaving only tranquillity.

The Fine-Material World

In the Sensuous Worlds, pleasant and unpleasant experiences result from the five senses, but in the worlds above it, pleasures result from the mind. This is the Fine-Material World or Rupa-Loka. Its name refers to the fact that those who reside there have material form, but it is of a finer and purer nature than the bodies of those existing in lower realms. There are sixteen realms within the Fine-Material World, each with its own requirements and features. These worlds are only accessible through meditation, or *jhana*.

The term 'born' is used in a different context when referring to 'birth' in these realms. It is perhaps better understood as 'came into being' rather than a physical birth, since the beings of these realms do not have physical bodies in the same sense as mortals on earth. Those who come into being in these worlds do so at the instant their mortal body dies on earth. They have the Six Entrances – the senses of sight, hearing, touch, taste and smell, plus a mind to comprehend the sensations they experience – but the amount of matter that makes up their form is less than a single atom.

The first of the worlds within Rupa-Loka is Brahma-Parisajja Deva, meaning the 'Retinue of Brahma'. Brahma is a deity inherited from Hinduism, though the name can have various applications. In Hinduism, Brahma is often credited or associated with the creation of the universe, but this is not so in Buddhism. Brahma remains important, as a protector of Buddhism and leader of the Devas. At times, the term Brahma is used to refer to any Deva who resides in this realm.

Above Brahma-Parisajja Deva is Brahma-Purohita Deva, home to the ministers of Brahma, and above that is Maha Brahma. This realm is home to greater Brahmas, one of whom is the ruler of the Brahma worlds. This being is powerful and benevolent, protecting the teachings of the Buddha, but suffers from the delusion that he is the creator of the universe. Unaware that there are planes higher than his own, the great Brahma believes he sits at the pinnacle of the universe. In fact, Maha Brahma is the highest of the worlds attainable with the first *jhana*, but there are many more discernible to those who practise correct meditation.

Among the planes the Great Brahma is unaware of are those accessible by the second *jhana*. These include Abhasvara Deva, Appamanabhara Deva and Parittabha Deva. The Devas of Abhasvara radiate light from their bodies and constantly emit cries of joy as they experience the delight of their existence. Most sources state that this realm is where beings are reborn after the destruction of the world, while they await a new world to inhabit. Appamanabhra is home to Devas of streaming radiance, whereas those of Parittabha emit 'limited radiance'.

This progression from more to less ostentation on higher planes fits with the general Buddhist mindset that more requires less – in other words, that those who are truly great do not need to show it off, and those who are wise grow also humble. The next group of worlds can be attained by those who have the third *jhana*. The lowest of them is Parittasubha Deva, the realm of limited glory (or aura). Next is Appamanasubha Deva, the realm of unbounded glory (or aura), and Subhakinna Deva, the realm of refulgent glory.

Above these worlds are those that can be attained by the fourth *jhana*. The first is Vehapphala Deva, home to very fruitful Devas. It is possible to be reborn in the realms of the hungry ghosts or animals, or even in hell, after a mediocre existence in this realm.

BELOW: Buddha visited the home of the gods to consult with and even teach them. In this depiction from the Preah Prom Rath monastery in Siem Reap, Cambodia, Buddha is visiting Brahma and Indra.

The highest of this group of worlds is Asannasatta, which is often described as the world of unconscious or mindless beings. Those who dwell here or are able to reach this realm through meditation have form but no thoughts or perceptions. They exist only as long as they can maintain this state of passive being, although the Devas of this realm are said to be able to live for five hundred aeons.

The next five worlds are the Pure Abodes, which can only be attained by 'non-returners'. These are individuals who have transcended their ties to the cycle of rebirth. Those who have left behind the 'five lower fetters' are known as Anagami. They are reborn in these lands and will attain nirvana there. Those who have cast off all ten fetters to samsara and whose self is free of spiritual pollutants are known as Arhat in Sanskrit and Arahant in Pali. This is a term for the Buddha and the best of his disciples. The term translates as 'pure one' or 'worthy one'.

BELOW: The city of Polonnaruwa in Sri Lanka is now a UNESCO World Heritage site. Its ruins include magnificent Buddhist statuary.

Realm Names

Most realm names contain the word Deva, which means that those who dwell there are supernatural beings rather than mortals. Although Deva also means god or god-like creature, the context here is slightly different. Not all the Devas of the higher worlds act like the gods of other religions. Many do nothing at all except 'be' in their realm, and are defined by the nature of the realm rather than possessing individual characteristics.

BELOW: The 'Offering of the Six Devas' in Hong Kong is a group of statues depicting gods making offerings to Buddha.

THE IMMATERIAL WORLD, OR ARUPA-LOKA, IS HOME TO BEINGS OF PURE MIND. IT IS ATTAINABLE BY THOSE WHO DIE WHILE MEDITATING IN THE FORMLESS *JHANAS*.

Aviha Deva is the realm of Devas Not Falling Away, which translates loosely to the understanding that those who have attained this level do not descend into the lower worlds but may continue to rise through the other Pure Abodes. The next of these is Atapa Deva, home to Devas who are untroubled by any events or cares. Sudassa Deva is the home of beautiful Devas and above this is Sudassi Deva, home to clear-sighted beings. The highest of the five Pure Abodes is Akanittha Deva, home to peerless Devas.

The Immaterial World

The Immaterial World, or Arupa-Loka, is home to beings of pure mind. It is attainable by those who die while meditating in the formless *jhanas*. The first of these worlds is Akasanañcayatanupaga Deva, or Infinite Space. The second is Viññanañcayatanupaga Deva, or infinite consciousness. Above this is Akiñcaññayatanupaga Deva, a world of nothingness. The highest of all the Immaterial Worlds is Nevasaññanasaññayatanupaga Deva, which can be translated as 'neither perception nor non-perception'.

Multiworld and Temporal Cosmology

Sources differ on the exact nature of the cosmos. Some postulate the existence of millions of worlds. This does not contradict the cosmology described above, as these worlds are within the realms already described or are parallel versions of them. This correlates to the existence of innumerable planets in our own universe; each is a separate world but part of the same vast realm.

There are other parallels to modern science to be found in Buddhist cosmology. Where the spacial cosmology described above explains the different realms and how they interact, temporal cosmology is concerned with how these realms come to exist and how they are destroyed. A complete cycle of creation and destruction takes place over a *maha-kalpa*, whose duration is billions of years at the very least.

Within the *maha-kalpa* are four periods known as *asankya-kalpas*. During the first of these, the world is formed. During the second, the universe is in a stable state. The third sees the universe proceeding towards destruction, while the fourth is a quiet period of nothingness after everything is destroyed.

This is consistent with modern scientific explanations of the origins of the universe. The Big Bang theory states that all energy and matter were concentrated at a single point before exploding out to fill the vacant universe. This energy and matter began in extremely simple forms but gradually coalesced into more complex structures, which became the building blocks of our universe.

ABOVE: This Tibetan map of the cosmos centres on Sumeru (Mount Meru), and shows the four continents lying in the Cosmic Ocean. Each of these has a distinctive shape – square, semicircular, circular and 'cart shaped'.

Buddhist texts refer to a formless universe gradually gaining solidity and form during the first stage in the cycle of creation and destruction, known as Vivartakalpa. During this *kalpa*, the primordial wind blows the wreckage of the old universe together. The details vary depending on how the old world was destroyed, but by the end of the Vivartakalpa, the cosmos has reached a stable state. Humans and other beings exist during this *kalpa*, albeit in the form of disembodied entities that emit light and move around at will.

As the universe becomes more solid, these entities take an interest and explore. This leads to the first cravings and a gradual move towards a form with solid bodies, gender differences and a need to eat. This in turn influences the development of the universe, since everything is linked to everything else, and sets the cosmos on an inevitable path to destruction. It is notable that during the Vivartakalpa, beings are reborn into a lower world than they previously inhabited. Essentially, those who did not achieve nirvana and leave the cycle of samsara lose part of their score but can play again.

BELOW: Amitabha, one of the Transcendent Buddhas, presides over the Pure Land of Sukhavati. Being reborn there is a stepping stone to enlightenment desired by those who struggle to follow the Dharma in the mortal realm.

The Buddha would not answer questions about the exact process that caused the creation of the world. He used the analogy of a man shot with a poisoned arrow who wants to know all about the arrow, the poison, the shooter and his reasons for shooting, but will die before he finds out the answers. The implication is that some things are unknowable to mortals, who would be better advised to spend their time dealing with the questions that can be answered in their lifetimes.

During the second *asankya-kalpa*, known as Vivartasthayikalpa, the universe is stable enough for people to live in. This does not mean it is static. Indeed, the only constant is change. Human lifetimes begin as extremely short, extending to enormous lengths as the world is improved by people performing good and ethical acts. This takes place, as with each *asyanka-kalpa*, over twenty *antah-kalpas*. Between each is a devastating war or period of violence, with an era of civilization and high morality in between. Human lifespans increase from ten years at the beginning of the *kalpa* to eighty thousand years at its end.

The third *kalpa* is Samvarakalpa, during which the world gradually degenerates. Lifespans become shorter, eventually dropping to just ten years, and the world becomes increasingly unpleasant to endure. Again, there are correlations to at least some modern scientific theories. The 'heat death' concept, whereby energy becomes evenly spread through the cosmos, does not appear to match the idea of destruction and reconstruction but the 'big crunch' theory does. Gravitational effects eventually halt the

expansion of the universe and contraction begins, finally leading to all matter and energy being concentrated at a single point. This paves the way for the next Big Bang and the expansion of a new universe in a never-ending cycle.

The fourth *kalpa* is known as Samvartasthayikalpa, a period of stillness that can be compared to the modern 'heat death' concept. Nothing at all happens in the realms below the Abhasvara worlds until the end of the aeon. Then, when the primordial wind begins to blow the wreckage back together, a new cycle can finally begin.

ABOVE: A map of Manusyaloka, or Manusa-Gati, the human world. It is a complex place, beset with contradictions and setbacks but these are necessary if a being is to have the experiences that might permit eventual enlightenment.

ABOVE: The Borobudur temple complex in Java is an UNESCO World Heritage site. Its layout broadly parallels the three layers of Buddhist cosmology: the heavens, the earthly realm and the underworlds.

OPPOSITE: A depiction of the wheel of life, with images of the changes and conditions a person might experience during their earthly existence. Buddhism accepts that life is confusing, and offers a way to find some answers.

The manner of destruction visited upon the world follows a strict cycle. Seven times the world will be destroyed by fire, and on the eighth by water. The cycle is then repeated seven times. The next destruction is by wind, after which the whole cycle repeats itself. Which of the higher realms are affected depends on the nature of destruction. The fires that consume the world do not reach the Abhasvara worlds, but the floods that follow every seventh universal conflagration do. The floods destroy everything below the world of Vehapphala Deva, while the final destruction of the great cycle, accomplished by wind, reaches all the way to the Subhakinna Deva world, eliminating everything below. Only the formless realms and the worlds attainable through the fourth *jhana* are preserved.

The entire cycle of cycles is a natural process, which proceeds without the actions of gods or other powerful beings – and indeed despite anything anyone could do to stop it. Those who fail to achieve nirvana and leave the cycle are doomed to repeat it forever.

2

LIFE OF THE BUDDHA

The word 'Buddha' describes a state of being but can also be used to refer to a specific individual who has achieved it. There have been multiple Buddhas and there will be more in the future. As a result, there are statues and images of individuals with markedly different appearances, and references to people living across a long time span. There is not one that can be identified simply as the Buddha.

Given the cyclical nature of the universe in Buddhist beliefs, and the importance of reincarnation, it is possible to be confused into thinking that all the Buddhas must be reincarnations of the same person. This is absolutely not the case. Nor is Buddha a god or supernatural creature. Buddha was a human who transcended the cycle of samsara by achieving enlightenment. His teachings show others how to do the same and how to live better lives in the interim, but by definition the Buddha cannot be reincarnated.

OPPOSITE: The Lumbini grove in southern Nepal is generally accepted as the birthplace of Buddha. It is today a UNESCO World Heritage site and a destination for pilgrims.

Bodhisattva

Originally, the status of Bodhisattva was open only to males, but this changed over time. What has not changed is the requirement to be selfless and to help others. A Bodhisattva possesses a state of mind called *bodhicitta*, which consists of two essential components. In the absolute sense, the individual embodies enlightenment; it is their very nature rather than a poise or adopted attitude. In the relative sense, their mind must constantly be directed towards enlightenment and the maintenance of this state.

BELOW: Bodhisattva Avalokiteshvara, who is known in China as Guanyin, is the personification of compassion.

His status as Buddha breaks the cycle of samsara and frees him from the burden of returning to an earthly life that is filled with suffering.

Buddha was born into a noble household in what is now southern Nepal. Scholars are divided as to exactly when this was. Some give his lifetime as 568–483 BCE, others around a century later. There are also claims that Buddha in fact lived much more recently. Most of what is known about his life was only recorded centuries later. Until that time, the story of Buddha's enlightenment and subsequent teachings was passed down as oral tradition, and multiple variants now exist.

Previous Lives of the Buddha

Accounts of the life of Buddha were compiled from often fragmentary information. Some focus entirely on Siddhartha Gautama, while others begin long before he was born. In these accounts, the being who would go on to become the Buddha set out on his path in the ancient past and lived many lives before finally being reincarnated as Siddhartha Gautama.

In the distant past, a member of the priestly Brahmin caste, whose name is sometimes given as Sumedha, began to seek answers about the nature of the cosmos. He took the path of the ascetic, living a lonely life of meditation and self-denial. His mystical powers – often referred to as Yogic powers – developed, allowing him to fly around the world seeking wisdom. Eventually, he happened upon a man named Dipamkara who was engaged in teaching.

Humbly approaching Dipamkara, Sumedha learned that he was a Buddha. Sumedha stayed with Dipamkara Buddha and learned all he could, soon realizing that he could attain enlightenment quickly and leave the cycle of samsara. Instead, he vowed to take a much longer path, so that he might help others attain nirvana. Dipamkara Buddha told Sumedha that the name of his final incarnation would be Gautama, along with many details about his followers and the circumstances of his enlightenment.

Dipamkara was one of the Buddhas of the past, and was followed by others who were encountered by reincarnations of Sumedha. Each time, he vowed to them that he would proceed on his own long road to Buddhahood. After his penultimate life as Prince Vessantara, Buddha was reborn in the realm of Tusita Deva, from where he searched for a suitable place to begin his final incarnation. By this time, he had accumulated enormous amounts of virtue as a result of living many good lives and was ready to become Siddhartha Gautama.

ABOVE: One requirement for status as a Buddha is the ability to recognize a future Buddha. In the case of Dipankara Buddha, depicted here, it was the future Gautama Siddhartha.

The Early Life of Siddhartha Gautama

According to tradition, Siddhartha Gautama was a nobleman of the Shakya clan. However, there is some doubt surrounding the status of his parents. His father, Suddhodana, is sometimes referred to as a prince or king, but the Shakya state was in fact an oligarchic republic. It was ruled by a council of high-ranking Kshatriya, or warriors, who elected a raja as their head. As such, it is probably incorrect to describe Suddhodana as a king.

The Shakya homeland lay north of the Ganges River, away from the major centres of civilization, and was a vassal state of the Kingdom of Kosala. India at the time was not a unified

RIGHT: King Suddhodana and his attendants, depicted on the Great Stupa at Sanchi in Madhya Pradesh, India.

country but a patchwork of small kingdoms and tribal areas. The dominant religion was what today would be called Hinduism. Like India itself, Hinduism was not a unified religion. There were many holy writings, some of them contradictory, and rather than presenting a set of concrete answers to the mysteries of the universe, Hinduism encouraged its adherents to live a good life and ponder deep questions.

Twelve years before the birth of Buddha, the Brahmins – priests – told his father that the coming child would be a great ruler or a wise sage. The latter did not appeal, since sages were penniless ascetics who wandered the world seeking wisdom, so Buddha's father resolved to prevent this.

His son would have the best of everything and be protected from the world's ills; he would be educated to rule and thus channelled in the direction in which his father wanted him to go.

Years later, Maha Maya – wife of Raja Suddhodana – dreamed that a white elephant with six tusks had entered her womb. She correctly took this to mean that she had conceived a child who was destined for greatness, and ten months later, she gave birth in an unusual manner. While walking in the garden of Lumbini, Maha Maya grasped the branch of a sal tree, whereupon the baby emerged from under her right arm. She subsequently died, just seven days later, and was reborn in the Tavatimsa Deva world.

The child was named Siddhartha, which translates from Sanskrit as 'he who achieves his aim', with the family name Gautama. He could walk and talk immediately, announcing that he had been born to seek enlightenment for the good of all and that this was his last incarnation. The child was clearly destined for great things, which was further confirmed when he was visited by Asita, an ascetic who advised Suddhodana and who had predicted Siddhartha's destiny. Although a notable figure himself, Asita paid homage to the child, and Suddhodana did likewise.

Sages

While most people lived a normal life balancing spiritual and earthly concerns, ascetics were common in India. Renouncing worldly things, these holy men often wandered the earth seeking knowledge and insight. The greatest of them were known as Rishis, or sages, and were said to have attained supernatural powers by meditation and self-denial.

BELOW: There are similarities between a Rishi, or sage, and an Arhat. Both may be able to wield incredible supernatural powers and have great wisdom, and both have renounced the mundane world.

ABOVE: **King Suddhodana was informed by the Brahmins that his child was destined for greatness. He tried to choose the path of kingship for his son, but was struggling against the forces of destiny.**

Later, while still a child, Siddhartha sat under a jambu tree in order to mediate. The tree's shadow remained still all day to protect him from the fierce sun and he was discovered by his father hovering cross-legged above the ground.

Despite these obvious signs that Siddhartha was destined for something other than kingship, Suddhodana continued to guide him towards a career as a monarch. The young prince was raised in luxury and kept isolated from the sufferings of the outside world. In addition to a good education, Siddhartha was trained in the arts of war. He learned swordsmanship and the noblest of Indian fighting skills, archery.

In order to keep his son distracted, Raja Suddhodana built three palaces for him. One was for the spring, one for the rainy season and one for the winter. He filled these palaces with the best of everything and, more importantly, removed everything bad. Monks, other than Siddhartha's teachers, were not permitted close to the palaces, and anyone who was seriously ill was taken elsewhere. Thus, the prince did not encounter teachings that might tempt him away or see upsetting sights that could cause him to question his way of life.

This was not entirely successful, so Suddhodana decided to provide a further distraction. He therefore decided to find Siddhartha a suitable wife. The prince had high standards, though they did not necessarily match the expectations of his station. Most young men of his rank might want to marry the daughter of a rich man, but Siddhartha did not care who the girl's parents were or what her social class might be. He wanted someone honourable and good.

Invitations were issued to eligible young women who met the prince's requirements. Many visited the palace before Yasodhara caught his attention. She was the daughter of King Suprabudda, whose sisters Maya and Prajapati were married to Raja Suddhodana. Marriage between cousins was common in the noble houses of India at the time, and the choice was entirely agreeable to Suddhodana.

King Suprabudda was less impressed. He thought Siddhartha was rather soft and would not be a good ruler, not that he would be able to protect his kingdom or his wife from the threats they would inevitably face. Rather than agreeing outright to the wedding, Suprabudda organized a tournament that attracted five hundred entrants, including Siddhartha. The prize was to be marriage to Yasodhara.

BELOW: A Tibetan depiction of the palace in which Siddhartha Gautama spent his early life. His father tried hard to insulate the young prince from the unpleasant aspects of the outside world.

ABOVE: The bow was the noblest of weapons for an Indian prince. Siddhartha was also an accomplished wrestler, swordsman and horseman.

The training Siddhartha had received in horsemanship, fighting and similar warlike pursuits might have been in part intended to distract him from asking metaphysical questions, but he had excelled all the same. No one could match his prowess in the physical challenges and, when mental tests were presented, he naturally impressed even the sceptical Suprabudda. Convinced now of Siddhartha's worthiness, the king agreed to the marriage.

Historical data from this period is patchy at best. No written records were made until centuries after the death of Buddha. By that time, the story may have become garbled or later chroniclers might have interpreted it according to the norms of their time. Thus, references to kings, princes and even places may have been added later. Similarly, the neat and specific numbers of people involved are undoubtedly a

Buddhism and Hinduism

As a young man, Siddhartha Gautama was taught many subjects by wise and knowledgeable individuals. Hinduism was the dominant religion in the region, so Siddhartha would have been familiar with the many gods. His enlightenment changed his perspective on the Hindu deities but they were still recognized and respected. Part of his philosophy must also have originated from his Hindu education. One of its key principles is the absence of simple and easy answers. Instead, adherents are expected to ask difficult questions and seek their own understanding.

storytelling device. It is rather unlikely that exactly ten thousand messengers were sent, nine times over, but the overall impression is evident – great efforts were made to persuade the Buddha to come home.

While the exact details are open to question, the overall story is clear. Siddhartha Gautama lived in luxury and wanted for nothing. He had a beautiful wife and a comfortable home life. Indeed, it was artificially comfortable. Siddhartha might encounter someone who was ill, but never someone who was dying. Thus, he developed a skewed vision of the world in which there was little suffering and a great deal of joy. This changed when he ventured out into the wider world, but it may be that he was already wise enough to suspect he was being deceived.

ABOVE: Yasodhara was absolutely devoted to her husband. When he left to become a monk, she followed the same practices and ultimately became a member of his religious community.

The Great Renunciation

It had been prophesied that Siddhartha Gautama would leave his palace after witnessing a sick man, an old man and a wandering priest. His father tried to avoid this, but eventually the prince decided to venture out of his palace and see the world for himself. He asked his charioteer, a man named Chandaka in Sanskrit and Channa in Pali, to take him out. They made four trips. On each of them, Siddhartha Gautama witnessed one of what became known as the Four Great Signs.

On the first trip, Siddhartha saw a man who looked different from the others he had seen. This man was unable to stand up straight and was tottering along with the aid of a stick. Siddhartha asked his charioteer what this man had done that he was so afflicted, and the charioteer explained that this was the effect of old age. Siddhartha wondered if he, too, would become aged and feeble. The charioteer confirmed that he would, and Siddhartha was dismayed.

Cutting his excursion short, the prince returned to his palace to think about what he had seen. He decided that birth was not

ABOVE: On his journeys outside the palace, Siddhartha Gautama encountered sickness, old age and death. His charioteer had the awkward task of explaining these concepts to the sheltered young prince.

as joyous as he had thought, since it doomed anyone born to a fate of old age and infirmity. While he gloomily pondered this revelation, his charioteer told his father what had happened. Suddhodana was determined that his son remain at the palace and ordered that he be surrounded by pleasant distractions.

After a while, Siddhartha decided to go out again. Along the way, he saw a man who was suffering from severe disease. People were trying to help him but to no avail. Siddhartha asked his charioteer why this man looked different from the others, and was informed that he suffered from an illness. Siddhartha did not understand, and asked if the man would recover. His charioteer informed him that it was highly unlikely. Upon learning that illness could strike anyone, Siddhartha returned in sadness to his palace. There, he again denounced birth, since it condemned people to a life that could be blighted in this manner. The charioteer dutifully answered Suddhodana when he asked about the trip, and Suddhodana was once more concerned. He ordered that Siddhartha's life be made as pleasant as possible, and for the time being the prince remained in his palace.

Eventually, Siddhartha decided to go out again. His charioteer drove him among the parks so that he could be delighted by their beauty, but this time they encountered a funeral. Siddhartha did not know about death, and wanted to take a closer look. When he did so, his charioteer had to explain that people die and will never be seen again by those who love them. He confirmed that Siddhartha himself, and everyone he cared about, would die sooner or later.

Again, Siddhartha returned to his chambers and pondered what he had seen. Life seemed to him to be a bitter thing, cursed with illness, old age and death. His charioteer reported the incident and Suddhodana ordered that still more pleasure and distraction be heaped upon his son. This worked for a time, but eventually Siddhartha left the palace a fourth time.

This time, Siddhartha and his charioteer encountered a man with a shaven head wearing a yellow robe. The charioteer explained that this was a monk, who had left behind the distractions of a normal life and become a homeless wanderer. Siddhartha was intrigued and approached the monk to learn more. The monk repeated what the charioteer had already told Siddhartha, that he had gone forth into a new life of good and peaceful deeds. He explained how he lived, and Siddhartha understood what he must do.

Ordering Chandaka to return home without him, Siddhartha cut off his hair and put on the yellow robe. Thereby, he went forth in search of wisdom and answers to his questions. The

LEFT: In some versions of the tale, Siddhartha Gautama sent his charioteer back with his possessions and slipped away. In other tales, he returned to see his sleeping wife and child before making his Great Departure.

ABOVE: Siddhartha Gautama's Great Departure was complicated by the decision of sixty-four thousand other people to go with him. Ultimately, he had to leave them behind to pursue his ascent to enlightenment.

charioteer naturally reported the incident to Raja Suddhodana, and everyone else in Kapilavatthu heard about it. Since their prince had gone forth, they decided to do the same. Sixty-four thousand inhabitants of Kapilavatthu shaved their heads, donned yellow robes and followed Siddhartha.

For a time, Siddhartha tried to live the life of an itinerant recluse with this vast horde of followers around him. It soon became apparent, though, that he was never going to achieve wisdom with so many people following him about the countryside. After parting company with all his followers, he was able to meditate and ponder the questions that beset him. Life was inevitably marred by suffering: old age, illness and death. There seemed to be no way to escape, but he resolved to find one.

In some versions of the tale, Siddhartha does not leave his old life behind immediately, and instead makes the decision at the palace. He silently bids his sleeping wife and child farewell and slips away in the middle of the night to prevent his father from interfering. In this variant, Siddhartha is assisted in his departure by the faithful charioteer, who takes his clothing and jewellery back to the palace. No matter the circumstances of the departure, Siddhartha made a huge and difficult decision to leave behind not only a comfortable life but also the people he loved.

Early Teachers

Siddhartha Gautama learned from everyone he could, encountering many different beliefs and viewpoints. He began with Hinduism, the dominant religion of the time. There were plenty of wise Hindu teachers to learn from, and they had a great deal of wisdom to offer. He also sought out those who followed the Jain religion. When he had exhausted these possibilities, Siddhartha turned to other holy men.

ALMS AND THE HOLY MAN

It was common in those times to offer food to mendicants. These were holy men who were respected and sometimes feared; some were said to bestow fearsome curses upon those who offended them. In any case, a wandering ascetic asked for little and would be satisfied with the simplest of meals. Indeed, Siddhartha would refuse food that had been cooked specially for him. Only the most basic and often unappetizing food could be accepted. This was part of the mendicant lifestyle, a necessary renunciation of all pleasant things.

BELOW: Ordinary people would want to honour a visiting holy man by offering him a good meal, but Siddhartha Gautama would accept only the simplest of foods, in keeping with his ascetic lifestyle.

ABOVE: Buddha learned a great deal from Udraka Ramaputra and eventually surpassed him. However, he could not learn all he needed from one or two teachers, so he continued his wanderings.

Two teachers in particular influenced his early development. The first was Arada Kalama, who taught Siddhartha how to enter a meditative state known as *jhana*. Freeing his mind of other considerations, the mystic would concentrate upon a thought or object and gain wisdom. Siddhartha excelled and gained wisdom. Despite being invited to remain with Arada Kalama, co-teaching his three hundred disciples, Siddhartha declined. While he had learned much, he had not achieved his goal of enlightenment.

Next, Siddhartha studied under Udraka Ramaputra, who taught him other forms of meditation. In a state neither of perception nor of non-perception, Siddhartha learned much. He mastered meditation to such a degree that Udraka asked to become his student, but Siddhartha chose to continue his wanderings, as he had not attained enlightenment. Instead, he travelled with five companions and inflicted terrible denials upon his body. For six years, Siddhartha practised extreme austerities, at times eating only a single grain of rice a day. Occasionally, he allowed himself to eat more, or else he had only one meal a fortnight. By depriving his body, he sought to free his mind.

It was not this extreme lifestyle that caused Siddhartha's companions to leave him but its abandonment. Nearing death

due to starvation, he accepted a bowl of rice. After he had eaten, he realized his current path was not leading where he wanted. After years of extreme asceticism, he had not attained enlightenment, but he had become wise enough to understand that a different approach was necessary. His companions preferred to stay on the path of privation and self-denial, and parted company with Siddhartha when he went into a village in search of a more substantial meal than a single grain of rice.

Other versions of the tale state that Siddhartha was offered milk and honey by a woman named Sujata, and that this restored his strength. Either way, he understood that self-denial could only take him so far. While his friends continued with their austerities, Siddhartha began to eat properly and became physically stronger. He would later teach that the body must be properly nourished in order to support the quest for mental and spiritual enlightenment.

Enlightenment

Self-denial was a common practice among holy men. By depriving their bodies, they freed their minds, sometimes developing Yogic (psychic) powers that could be maintained

ABOVE: Each Buddha attained enlightenment meditating under a tree. In the case of Siddhartha Gautama, it was a sacred fig tree. One still stands at the same location, probably an offspring of the original.

by further austerities. Extreme self-denial was in many ways the default option, and Siddhartha would have known it produced results. However, those results were not the ones he needed.

The decision to take another road would have been a difficult one, especially since it may have looked like giving up or flinching from what needed to be done. Such thoughts were driven by ego and might be a distraction, so after careful consideration, Siddhartha embarked upon his 'middle path' between luxury and austerity. He had now known both, and understood that neither led to enlightenment.

Siddhartha bathed in the River Nairanjana and made his way to the Bodhi tree; a sacred fig tree that grew in Bodh Gaya, in what is today the Indian state of Bihar. Siddhartha seated himself under the tree and closed his eyes, pondering upon all he had learned. For six days, he remained there, unmoving and deep in meditation, until realization burst upon him.

The revelation was a simple yet profound one. Enlightenment could not be found in all the teachings of the sages or in deprivation and meditation, because it had never been lost. Enlightenment was the natural state of all beings. Unhappiness and suffering came from the feeling of lacking enlightenment, but all things had within them the ability to return to their state of enlightenment.

The former prince opened his eyes and gazed upon the morning star, and became the Buddha, or Awakened One. He was free from suffering, and for several weeks he enjoyed the peace and tranquillity of his enlightened state. At first, he decided not to try to teach others about what he had discovered, as it was unlikely they would understand. However, Buddha eventually perceived he had a duty to help others as much as he could and sought out his former teachers to share his knowledge.

Both Arada Kalama and Udraka Ramaputra died just days before Buddha found them, but he was able to seek out the five ascetics who had shared his early wanderings. At first, they were unreceptive; they had held true to their path of meditation and suffering when Siddhartha turned aside. However, they were wise enough to soon recognize there was something special and different about Buddha, and welcomed him. These five ascetics were the first to benefit from the Buddha's wisdom.

BELOW: Buddha's first sermon was to the five ascetics who had been his companions. They were won over by his wisdom, turning aside from their path and on to his.

Leading the Sangha

Word of Buddha's great wisdom spread quickly. He became known as Shakyamuni, the Sage of the Shakyas, after his clan. Many more followers came

GAUTAMA BUDDHA COULD HAVE REMAINED IN ONE PLACE, ATTRACTING FOLLOWERS TO HIS SANGHA AND TEACHING TO LARGE NUMBERS. THIS WAS NOT HIS WAY, AND INSTEAD HE WANDERED FOR MANY YEARS AMONG THE ORDINARY PEOPLE OF INDIA.

to join the original five. These formed a Sangha, or community, who followed the teachings of Gautama Buddha and in turn taught others. At first they were all men, but in time, women and children would also join the Sangha.

Members of the Sangha were known as *bhiksus*, which translates as 'monks', and followed a similar lifestyle to the ascetics many of them had been. Their possessions were limited to a robe and a few necessities, which included a razor to shave their heads. This was a symbol of having left the mundane life behind to seek a life of meditation. Wandering in small groups or alone, they had no means to support themselves and relied on the charity of those they encountered.

Gautama Buddha could have remained in just one place, attracting followers to his Sangha and teaching to large numbers. This was not his way, and instead he wandered for many years among the ordinary people of India. He helped where he could and taught those who would listen. Some sources give a period of forty-nine years, others forty-five, during which Buddha taught everyone who would listen. During this period, he also returned to his home, where some members of his family renounced their courtly lives and joined his Sangha. His father, Suddhodana, did not, although he did receive Buddha's teachings.

As word of the Buddha's great wisdom spread, rulers and wealthy people gave gifts. Some of these were extensive parks, which could be used as religious retreats or centres of teaching. Buddha chose instead to continue his penniless wanderings. He meditated and taught, and others passed on his words. No written record of his words was made during his lifetime, but after his death, the five hundred most holy of his followers gathered to ensure they remembered all his teachings correctly. This became known as the First Council. Ananda, brother-in-law to Siddhartha Gautama and a loyal follower of the Buddha, recited all the discourses he had heard. These are the Sutras. The Vinaya, or two hundred and fifty rules governing Buddhist monks, were recited by Upali. The Abhidharma, the body of knowledge concerning the physical and metaphysical world, was recited by Mahahashyapa. These three bodies of work were written down for the first time; the Sutras, the Vinaya and the

Abhidarma collectively became known as the Tripitaka. This translates as 'Triple Baskets'.

The death of the Buddha was in keeping with his life. In the town of Kushinagara, he ate a meal – some sources say it was pork and others state mushrooms – and lay down on his side. He spoke with his closest followers for the last time and reminded them that everything is impermanent. The Dharma he had taught would guide and comfort them. With a final reminder to strive diligently, the Buddha died and left the cycle of rebirth.

In the years that followed, the religious communities attracted new followers while wandering monks taught those they met. The result was a gradual and probably uneven spread across India and beyond. People who had travelled might come into contact with Buddhist teachings and take them home, or more likely Buddhists would travel wherever they could and teach those they encountered. It is thus likely that Buddhism spread down the

ABOVE: Those who followed the Buddha renounced almost all worldly possessions except their alms bowls. This became a symbol of their status – penniless and reliant on the kindness of others.

major trade routes, notably the Silk Road, and expanded out from new centres established at stopovers and population centres.

The Family of Buddha

Buddha's close relatives fared well or badly according to how they reacted to his departure and subsequent enlightenment. His father, Suddhodana, knew that his son was destined for greatness and wanted him to be a magnificent king. There may have been an element of personal ego involved in this decision, or Suddhodana may have genuinely believed it was the best

LEFT: The death of Buddha might seem strangely mundane, but there was no need for grand gestures. He quietly departed the cycle of rebirth having completed his work and given others what they needed to follow him.

choice. A king would father a magnificent dynasty whereas an ascetic, however wise, would not provide Suddhodana with grandchildren. Whatever his precise motivation, Suddhodana firmly opposed the chain of events that led to the emergence of the Buddha.

Suddhodana represents one of the most serious obstacles faced by the Buddha, yet his actions were never malicious. He clearly loved his son and was sad when he went away, sending messengers to invite Siddhartha home. This measure failed when the messengers decided to join Buddha's growing community rather than return to the service of Suddhodana. A personal entreaty when Buddha returned home to visit was also ineffective. Nevertheless, Suddhodana was glad to see his son and welcomed him graciously.

Suddhodana's first attempt to prevent Siddhartha from becoming a monk was a little underhand. By providing luxuries and distractions, Suddhodana made sure his son had a lot to give up, perhaps making the decision harder. He also insulated Siddhartha from the ills and injustices of the world, which might have led to him never asking the big questions in the first place. Yet, once Siddhartha's feet were upon the path he had chosen, his father believed in him.

News came to the palace that Siddhartha had died as a result of the harsh self-denial he was practising. Suddhodana would have none of it, stating that Siddhartha would achieve his goal of enlightenment. If Suddhodana and the promise of a luxurious life could not persuade Siddhartha to turn aside, then death stood no chance. In this, he was correct; Siddhartha was alive and on the road to success. When the day came that the Buddha emerged, Suddhodana decided to send messengers inviting him to visit his former home. Ten thousand envoys set off, but they forgot about their mission when they heard the Buddha preach. Ten thousand more were subsequently sent, also to no avail, and ten thousand

BELOW: King Suddhodana sent a thousand carts full of supplies every day to support his son, along with messengers to invite him to come home. Instead, they joined the religious community and went wandering with the Buddha.

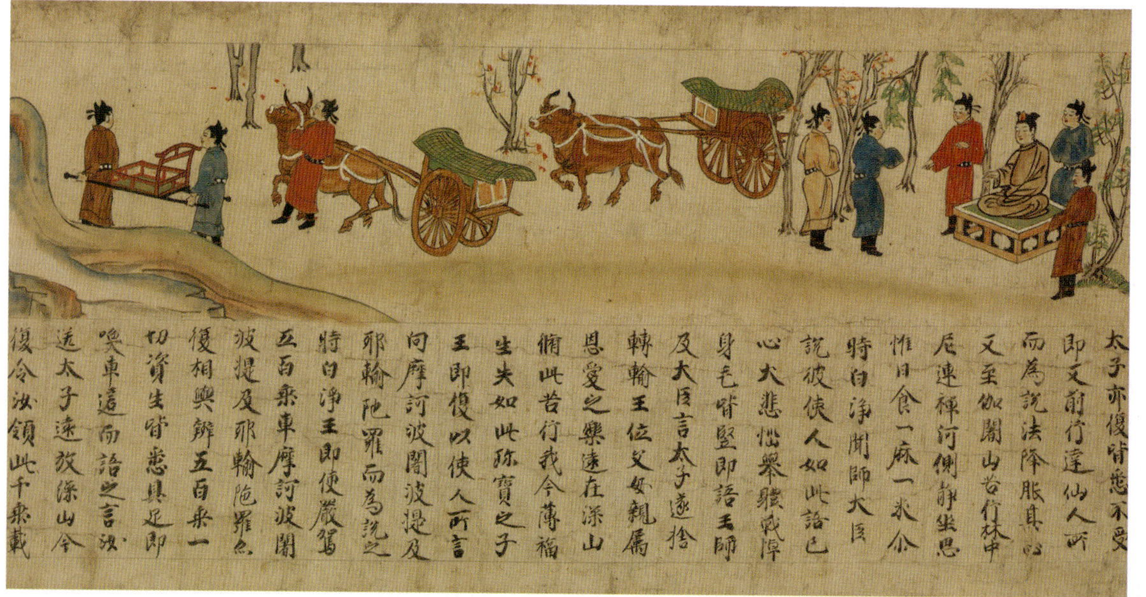

more. After the ninth attempt, Suddhodana tried something different. He sent Kaludayi, a boyhood friend of Siddhartha who had been born on the same day, with the invitation.

Kaludayi was the son of Suddhodana's closest advisor, and was given permission to join the Buddha's following on condition that he deliver the invitation. He did so, and in due course the Buddha came to Kapilavatthu. He begged for food in the streets as usual, which upset Suddhodana. The king quite reasonably wanted to know why his son was out begging when anything he wanted would be placed before him. There was no shortage of food at the palace; Suddhodana had sent Buddha a bowl of fruit on every one of the sixty days it took him to arrive at Kapilavatthu.

It might even have seemed a bit embarrassing – both as a host and a father – to see such an eminent man out begging in the street. The Buddha replied that begging is the custom of all like him. At this, Suddhodana began to understand some of Buddha's wisdom, and how much Siddhartha's worldview differed from his own. Upon hearing Buddha preach, he comprehended more and, at the end of his life, Buddha visited Suddhodana to teach what he needed to become enlightened.

Suddhodana influenced the spread of Buddhism as the inspiration of a rule. When Buddha was about to induct his own son Rahula and Suddhodana's son Nanda, he asked that other parents be spared the sadness he felt at losing his own children. Buddha agreed, ruling that no one should be ordained as a monk without the permission of their parents. Although Suddhodana had tried to prevent the Buddha's search for enlightenment, he came to understand that it was the right path and supported his son. In one of his sermons, Buddha revealed that Suddhodana had been his father in other lives, too, and had previously refused to believe that his son was dead despite being shown convincing evidence proving that he was.

ABOVE: Suddhodana, or indeed any of the nobles of the region, would have showered Buddha with riches if he had asked, but all he needed was a begging bowl and faith in the charity of others.

Siddhartha's wife Yasodhara was born on the same day as him. They were married at age sixteen, and had a son named Rahula. When Siddhartha went away to seek enlightenment, Yasodhara withdrew from court life and emulated the privations he suffered. Upon Buddha's return to his old home, the rest of the household wanted to see Siddhartha, but Yasodharawas was unsure whether she should. She was no longer his wife in any meaningful sense and wondered if he would want to see her.

In fact, Buddha did want to see Yasodhara, and was told she was in her room. He went to see her, finding her clothed in yellow robes as he was. Yasodhara had given up everything her husband had renounced, eating no more than he did and refusing the luxuries of the palace. The Buddha then revealed that Yasodhara had been his wife in previous incarnations and was just as devoted. She eventually joined the Buddha's religious community as a nun.

ABOVE: Siddhartha Gautama depicted with his wife Yasodhara and their son Rahula. Both would eventually follow him and become enlightened, though he never showed any particular favour towards people from his former life.

Prajapati, sister of Maha Maya and thus aunt to Siddhartha, was also married to Raja Suddhodana. She had taken care of Siddhartha when his mother died and he had grown up playing with her children. As well as being a parent to the young prince, Prajapati played an important part in the development of the Buddha's following. It was she who persuaded him to ordain women, becoming the first Buddhist nun. She is known to history as Mahaprajapati Gautami.

Siddhartha left his home soon after his child Rahula was born. The name translates as 'fetter', since the baby was born while Siddhartha was debating whether or not to leave the palace. His birth made the decision harder but perhaps more necessary, as Siddhartha knew his child would suffer and die like everyone else. The ability to provide some answers when Rahula needed them might have been a factor in the decision.

Siddhartha thus left his son in the care of Suddhodana's household, where he would live a comfortable and privileged life. When Siddhartha returned to visit, Rahula was about nine years old. He asked what he would inherit from his father. Rather than riches, the Buddha gave him knowledge and wisdom, causing Rahula to give up his life as a prince and follow his father.

Buddha was fair to his followers, and his relatives received no special treatment. When Rahula's dry sleeping-place was taken by an older monk during a rainstorm, Buddha simply checked he was safe and left him to get wet.

BELOW: After the death of Maha Maya, Siddhartha's mother, her sister Prajapati raised Siddhartha as her own child. She later became the first Buddhist nun after convincing Buddha to accept females into the Sangha.

RIGHT: Rahula was prone to all the follies of youth, including playing pranks on those coming to visit the Buddha. He accepted the lessons this earned him with good grace and went on to achieve enlightenment at a very young age.

However, Rahula was not always the best of monks. One day, he found it amusing to misdirect someone who was coming to see the Buddha. His father was not impressed, and taught him a wise lesson. Showing Rahula the small amount of water remaining in a dipper, he compared this to how much there was of a monk who felt no shame in lying. Next, he threw the water away, stating that whatever there was of a monk in someone who lied shamelessly could be discarded as easily. He turned the dipper upside down and compared this to whatever there was of a monk in someone who told such lies. Finally, he showed Rahula the hollow, empty dipper. This he compared to whatever there was of a monk in someone who told lies without shame.

This was a valuable and potent lesson, which caused Rahula to change his ways. The Buddha taught him how to reflect on how his words and actions might affect others, with remarkable results. Rahula is said to have achieved enlightenment at the age of eighteen. He was instrumental in his mother Yasodhara's decision to become a nun. He died young but is considered an inspiration to novice monks.

HIS FATHER-IN-LAW, SUPRABUDDA, WAS ANGERED THAT SIDDHARTHA WOULD ABANDON HIS WIFE AND THEIR YOUNG SON SO THAT HE COULD WANDER AROUND THE WORLD AS AN ASCETIC.

Hostile Relatives

Other family members, however, became opponents of the Buddha. His father-in-law, Suprabudda, was angered that Siddhartha would abandon his wife and their young son so that he could wander around the world as an ascetic. Eventually, he got his chance to do something about it when he heard Buddha and his followers were approaching. The ascetics intended to beg for food, which must have further confused and offended Suprabudda. Why would Buddha beg for what he was entitled to as a prince? Suprabudda confronted the band of ascetics and refused to allow them to pass. At this, they simply turned around and went elsewhere.

Whatever Suprabudda had intended to achieve, he brought about his undoing. Buddha stated that his father-in-law would be swallowed up by the earth for his disrespect. This would have been a frightening pronouncement, as sages were well known for their ability to deliver powerful curses. Certainly, Suprabudda took it seriously. He retired to a high part of the

ABOVE: **Although they were presumably rather bad characters, the assassins sent by Ajatashatru were overcome with remorse when they approached the Buddha and begged to join his following instead of carrying out their orders.**

palace and for a while refused to come down. However, he forgot his danger when he saw one of his horses was loose. Rushing to catch the escaped animal, he fell down the palace stairs and was consumed by the earth.

Suprabudda's two sons, Ananda and Devadatta, became followers of the Buddha. Ananda was loyal and a good friend to Buddha, whereas Devadatta was rather less so. He seems to have missed the point of at least some of Buddha's teachings, seeking to usurp power in the Sangha by devious means. Devadatta was friendly with Ajatashatru, a prince of Magadha. Perhaps getting a little above himself, he proposed that the Buddha retire and grant Devadatta leadership of the Sangha.

Devadatta was initially a good and worthy member of the community. He could wield psychic powers, suggesting he engaged in very harsh self-denial and powerful meditation. However, he could not achieve enlightenment. Perhaps this was his motivation when he pushed for stricter asceticism among the people of the Sangha, even though Buddha himself had abandoned extreme self-denial as unproductive.

Devadatta proposed some new rules for the members of the community. His suggestion that they must not eat fish or meat was entirely acceptable, but the other parts of his proposal were considered questionable. For instance, Devadatta thought that monks must live in the forest, at the foot of trees, and wear robes made out of discarded rags. They must not permit non-monks to give them clothing, and were expected to rely solely upon food given to them.

Buddha's response to this suggestion was distinctly mild. He replied that the members of the Sangha could follow these rules if they wished, but there was no requirement to do so. As to allowing Devadatta to replace him as leader, Buddha told

Devadatta plainly that he was not worthy to lead the community. These rejections angered Devadatta, who resorted to some extreme measures to get rid of his rival. First, he convinced his friend Ajatashatru to depose and kill his father, then he set about trying to murder Buddha.

The first attempt involved hired assassins sent by Ajatashatru. The plan was that two would kill Buddha, then four more would ambush and kill them to prevent the instigator from being discovered. The four would then be slain by yet more assassins just to make sure there was nobody left alive to talk.This plan had a fatal flaw. When the assassins approached Buddha, they were so impressed by him that they joined his Sangha instead of killing him.

Devadatta then tried the more direct method of rolling a large rock down a hillside to crush Buddha. He assumed that a rock could not be turned aside in the manner of people, but in that he was wrong. The rock broke apart before it could strike Buddha. Finally, Devadatta turned a maddened elephant loose near Buddha and his party. This failed the same way as the other plans; the elephant became calm and docile in Buddha's presence

BELOW: Devadatta, enemy of Buddha through multiple lifetimes, met a suitably bad end. Made ill by his misdeeds, he suffered greatly and was then swallowed up by the earth. Unable to leave the cycle of samsara, he was presumably reincarnated somewhere fairly unpleasant.

Accounts vary as to Devadatta's fate. Some versions state that several hundred members of the Sangha left with Devadatta and set up their own community. They were brought back by Moggallana and Sariputra, senior disciples of Buddha, who reminded them of the correct teachings. Devadatta himself was made ill by the burden of his foul deeds and sought a reconciliation with Buddha. He died before they could meet, but did repent of his actions. In some versions of the tale, he tried to find Buddha and apologize for his misconduct, but was swallowed up by the earth along the way.

3

THE JATAKA TALES

The Jataka tales are part of the Pali Canon: the holy writings of Buddhism. They tell of the previous lives of the Buddha before he was finally reborn as Siddhartha Gautama and achieved enlightenment. Each of the tales focuses on an aspect of the Buddha's teachings, with the Buddha featuring in various human and animal forms. In both Sanskrit and Pali, Jataka means 'birth'.

The Jataka tales primarily refer to their central character as Bodhisattva, which translates as 'one whose goal is awakening'. This is the being who will eventually become the Buddha after he passes through multiple incarnations. This was a choice on the part of the Buddha, who decided to take the long way around in order to help others achieve enlightenment. Other Bodhisattvas have existed, eventually becoming Buddhas with their own tales.

OPPOSITE: The Jataka tales are part of the essential canon of Buddhism. They illustrate elements of the teachings through incidents in previous lives of the Buddha.

ABOVE: The Valahassa Jataka tells the tale of how Buddha, in his incarnation as a magical flying horse, rescued shipwreck survivors from a town of deceitful she-goblins.

The Jataka tales relate some of the occasions when Bodhisattva helped people in his incarnations before Siddhartha Gautama. There are hundreds of tales, many dating from around 400–300 BCE. These were brought together in a collection known as Jataka-atthakatha. This has been attributed to a monk named Buddhagosa, but there is significant doubt surrounding the identity of the compiler.

The First Jataka Tale

The Jataka tales are not presented in any particular order. They deal with various incarnations of Bodhisattva in different human, godly and animal forms. Each tale is self-contained, meaning they can be read in any order, but some have common themes or are set in the same period of time. Some characters are incarnations of others, particularly friends and enemies from the lifetime of Siddhartha Gautama.

The first of the Jataka tales, known as Appanaka Jataka, concerns a time when Bodhisattva was incarnated as a merchant. On his journeys, he encountered another merchant, who was a particularly stupid young man. Both wanted to cross an area of desert, but knew that their many oxen and wagons would tear up the road and make it impassable if they both tried to transit at once. The young and foolish merchant went first, setting off with his long line of carts.

Somewhere in the wilderness, the merchant encountered a devious and malevolent being who told him about the plentiful water ahead. It stated that there was so much water that the best course of action would be to smash the water jars and lighten the wagons for a faster transit. Of course, there was no water ahead. Unable to drink or cook rice, the merchant and his men were weakened and became easy prey for an ambush. They were killed and eaten, and the ambushers settled down to wait for the next caravan.

Bodhisattva and his wagons approached the same place a few weeks later, and the ambushers tried the same ruse. Bodhisattva was not fooled, pointing out to his followers that there were no rainclouds or signs of rainfall ahead. They soon came upon the site of the massacre and made a fortified camp that night. Bodhisattva's caravan was strengthened with additional wagons and the best of the foolish merchant's goods.

In his final incarnation, Buddha revealed that the foolish merchant was an incarnation of Devadatta, who led some of the Buddha's followers astray much as he led his caravan to destruction. Those who were with Bodhisattva and returned home safely were incarnations of the Sangha members who remained faithful. Like other Jataka tales, this one can be seen as a metaphor or lesson to be learned; in this case, it is an illustration of the importance of following the directions of the Buddha.

LEFT: The Bodhisattva Avalokiteshvara is associated with infinite compassion, personifying Buddha's decision to delay his own attainment of nirvana and live the many lives of the Jataka tales in order to help others achieve it.

Karma and Rebirth

The concept of Karma and rebirth is illustrated by the tale of a vain woman. In this story, the wife of King Assaka had died. The king did not understand that this was an inevitable part of the cycle of life and rebirth, and was overcome with grief. The current incarnation of the Buddha had taken the path of an ascetic and gained impressive Yogic powers. Even from his far-off dwelling in the Himalayas, he saw the distressed king and decided to visit him.

As a powerful ascetic, Bodhisattva could naturally fly. This made it easy for him to reach the king's city, where he landed in the royal park. He was greeted by a young Brahmin, who answered his questions about the king. He sounded like a decent man and a good ruler, but Bodhisattva wanted to meet the king himself. The Brahmin conveyed his invitation and in due course the king arrived in his chariot.

The king wanted to know if Bodhisattva really did know where his wife had been reincarnated. Of course, he did. Bodhisattva informed the king that his queen had been reincarnated as a dung worm in the park in which they sat. This had occurred because she was vain and gloried in her own appearance instead of living a good and virtuous life.

The king wanted proof of this rather disappointing news, so Bodhisattva summoned two dung worms to him and granted one of them the power of human speech. She confirmed that she was indeed a reincarnation of the queen, and that in this life she cared nothing for her former husband. Indeed, she was now devoted to her new love, the other dung worm. King Assaka ceased

LEFT: The Apsaras are known as Hiten in Japan. They are female spirits who sing and dance for the entertainment of both gods and mortals.

wallowing in grief at this point, and soon afterwards he found a new wife to love. He returned to his duties as a good and righteous king, and Bodhisattva went back to his home in the Himalayas.

In this tale, Bodhisatva taught the king that it was necessary to accept the impermanence of all things, and to put aside the grief caused by craving what was gone. Only when he had done this could the king move on and find happiness.

ABOVE: **Nagas are often depicted with the heads of cobras, but may have the characteristics of other serpents depending on the culture creating the image.**

King Senaka and the Naga

In Indian mythology, Nagas were powerful supernatural beings who were sometimes at odds with the gods. They originally lived on the surface of the earth but were consigned to an underground realm when their numbers grew too great. Among them was a certain Naga king who became friends with the human King Senaka.

The Naga king was out in the mortal world seeking food when he was spotted by some boys. Thinking him an ordinary snake, they began beating him with sticks and clods of earth. King Senaka, passing by on his way to his royal park, chased the boys away. The grateful Naga gave him gifts of jewels in return for his kindness, and assigned one of his female Nagas to be lover and companion to King Senaka. He taught Senaka a magical charm to summon the female Naga if she strayed out of sight.

Some time later, the king was in his gardens with his lover when he realized she had disappeared. She had spotted a water snake and transformed herself into snake form in order to have sex with him. Not knowing this, King Senaka spoke the charm and summoned his lover. He was angered at her infidelity and struck her with a piece of bamboo. She returned to the Naga

LEFT: The god Indra is often conflated with or referred to as Sakra. He is an important figure in Buddhism who rules over the other Devas and the Trāyastriṃa heaven.

LEFT: The culture of the time and the region producing any given version of the Jataka tales is reflected in the choice of imagery. This nineteenth-century version presents a different appearance to earlier compilations, but the story is the same.

world and told her king of the incident, but claimed that she had been beaten for disobedience.

Angered, the Naga king sent four of his warriors to destroy King Senaka. They arrived just as Senaka was telling his wife about the incident. Overhearing how the Naga girl had been unfaithful to Senaka, and must have lied to her own king, the Naga warriors decided not to kill Senaka and returned to their realm. It seems that while it was acceptable for the married King Senaka to have a Naga lover, her own infidelity to him was offensive. Senaka seems entirely comfortable in expressing his indignation about the unfaithful lover to his own wife.

Be that as it may, the Naga king agreed with Senaka and was sorry he sent assassins to slay him. To make amends, he taught Senaka another charm. This one allowed him to comprehend all sounds, on condition that he must not teach this skill to anyone else or he would be burned to death. The king's new ability caused him to display behaviour considered rather strange by others. He overheard ants discussing some fragments of food that had fallen, and was amused that they thought entire cartloads of cake and molasses had spilled. The amorous plans of a pair of flies further amused him but, since nobody else could hear or understand the sounds, the king's laughter was baffling.

Worried that her husband had been laughing at her, Senaka's queen asked him what had amused him. He told her of the charm, and she requested he teach it to her. Even when he explained that teaching someone else the charm would kill him, Senaka's wife continued to ask. Her husband's death was an

THE GOATS RESPONDED BY POINTING OUT THAT THE ASSES WERE TIED TO A CHARIOT THEY HAD TO PULL AROUND ALL DAY, AND EVEN WHEN THEY WERE UNHITCHED THEY DID NOT SEEK TO ESCAPE. THIS, ALLEGED THE GOATS, WAS A GREATER STUPIDITY THAN THEIRS.

acceptable price for such magic – or perhaps she resented the Naga lover more than she let on.

King Senaka eventually relented, and boarded his chariot to go to his park. He fully expected to die, but the god Sakra took pity on him. Sakra was the king of the Trāyastriṃa realm and is often conflated with the Hindu god Indra. He was married to Suja, whose assistance he enlisted in saving Senaka. The two transformed themselves into goats and manifested before Senaka's chariot. However, they ensured they could not be seen by anyone other than the asses who pulled the chariot.

The goats began speaking to one another as if they were about to begin making love, which offended the asses. They chided the goats, calling them stupid and shameless, and urged them to find a secluded place. The goats responded by pointing out that the asses were tied to a chariot they had to pull around all day, and even when they were unhitched they did not seek to escape. This, alleged the goats, was a greater stupidity than theirs. They added that Senaka was even more stupid than the asses.

The asses wanted to know what that meant, and the goats explained that the king was throwing away his life for a particularly poor reason. Overhearing and understanding this, King Senaka requested an explanation, and the goats told him that he should renounce a desire that would cost his life. This seemed like a wiser course of action than teaching the charm to his wife and being consumed by flames, but Senaka had promised his wife he would do so.

King Senaka felt bound by his promise, but with the help of Sakra he came up with a way to get out of the deal without breaking his word. He told his wife that she must earn the charm in the usual way, which meant receiving a hundred lashes upon her back without making a sound. The queen wanted the charm very badly and agreed, but after receiving only two or three blows she said that she no longer wished to learn it. King Senaka pointed out that she was quite happy to send him to his death to learn the spell, but was not willing to pay a relatively small price herself. He had her whipped anyway, and afterwards dismissed her from his life. This rather convoluted tale features Bodhisattva during his incarnation as the god Sakra. It can be

LEFT: Yakshinis are female nature-spirits. Some are benign and serve the gods whilst others are mischievous, using their beauty to entice and deceive unwary humans.

ABOVE: Buddha and other holy figures are often depicted using certain distinct hand positions. Each symbolizes a concept or action such as teaching the Dharma. The disciples' hand positions denote prayer or adoration.

taken as a commentary on the way some people are willing to let others pay the price for what they want, but will ultimately defeat themselves. King Senaka did not ask for anything but earned his magic fairly, receiving it as a gift from a grateful friend in return for a good deed. His wife took an easier path towards something she craved and lost everything she had.

Reincarnation According to the Being's Nature

There are many magical creatures in Buddhist mythology. Among them are the Yaksha and Yakshini, male and female beings who guard hidden treasures and bestow gifts upon mortals. Not all of them are benevolent, however. One tale features a beautiful Yakshini with a taste for human flesh. She had been a human woman in a previous incarnation and had a lot of bad Karma. As a result, she was reincarnated as a malevolent Yakshini and continued to act according to her rather unpleasant nature in this new life.

Seeing a woman bathing first her child then herself, the Yakshini transformed herself into human form in order to steal the baby. Deceiving the mother, she was given permission to hold the baby and immediately tried to abduct him. The mother tried to get her child back, which attracted the attention of the Bodhisattva. Although he could undoubtedly see that the Yakshini was not what she seemed, Bodhisattva caused the two women to reveal their own nature.

A PERSON'S NEXT LIFE REFLECTS WHAT THEY DID IN THE PRESENT ONE, WHICH CAN LEAD TO A DOWNWARD SPIRAL UNTIL THEY CHANGE THEIR WAYS.

In that incarnation, Bodhisattva was a judge and suggested a solution to the dispute. He drew a line on the ground and ordered the women to seize the baby by the arms and legs. Whichever could pull the baby over the line could keep him. As soon as the contest started, the real mother let her child go. She was unable to hurt him, whereas the Yakshini was willing to inflict pain on a baby in order to win the tug-of-war.

Bodhisattva pointed out that the real mother would let her child go rather than hurt him, but bystanders were still confused. He then revealed the identity of the Yakshini, making reference to her red, unblinking eyes and cruelty towards the child. The baby was returned to his grateful mother and the Bodhisattva made the Yakshini reveal her intentions to eat him. He rebuked the Yakshini for continuing in the sinful ways of her previous incarnation and made her vow to live a better life.

Bodhisattva helped both women in this tale. He saved one from losing her child and put the other on a more positive path. If the Yakshini kept her vow she would have a more positive reincarnation next time around. This is an underlying principle of reincarnation – a person's next life reflects what they did in the present one, which can lead to a downward spiral until they change their ways.

Breaking the Cycle

In one of the tales, Bodhisattva is an ascetic who visits a nearby kingdom to obtain supplies. The king was gracious towards him, and asked that Bodhisattva put his son on the right track. The boy was a rather toxic individual, so Bodhisattva showed him

where that led. Walking in the gardens, he bade the prince eat a nearby leaf. This was mildly poisonous and tasted bad. The prince immediately spat it out and uprooted the plant to get rid of it. Bodhisattva told him that if the tree grew to full size, the poison would be deadly, and that the prince was like the growing plant. If he continued on his present path, he would be uprooted and disposed of.

The prince realized the error of his ways and became a better man, eventually succeeding his father as a good and righteous king. Buddha later explained that those who do evil deeds will suffer in their present life and the next, and will be reborn as those inclined to more evil. The only way to break the cycle is to become a better person, ensuring a more favourable rebirth as someone inclined to do good.

OPPOSITE: A Thangka is a traditional Tibetan Buddhist art form, painted on to fabric. This example illustrates the birth and life of the Buddha through previous incarnations.

Reincarnation in Animal Form

Some of the Jataka tales raise questions in addition to imparting wisdom. Among these is the tale of how Bodhisattva was reborn in the form of a golden mallard. Normally, rebirth as an animal is the fate of those who spend their lives in ignorance or an animal-like state of mind. It seems unlikely that the future Buddha would have done so, but nevertheless, he is reborn as an animal in some incarnations. It may be that to achieve enlightenment he needed to experience all manner of existences.

This tale begins with Bodhisattva at the end of a life in which he was a Brahmin. He left behind three daughters as well as his wife, all of whom had to rely upon the charity of others to survive. Meanwhile Bodhisattva was reborn as a beautiful golden mallard and could remember all of his previous incarnations.

BELOW: Excavation of Old Bagan, the ancient capital of Myanmar, at the beginning of the twentieth century revealed twin pagodas, each bearing terracotta depictions of scenes from the Jataka tales.

OPPOSITE: The May Cave at Kyzyl, China, contains images of birds and animals in addition to Buddhist scenes. The caves are the oldest such site in China and are now a UNESCO World Heritage site.

Visiting his former home and discovering the plight of his family, the mallard decided to help. He would give his family one of his golden feathers, and others later when they needed them. He revealed his identity and offered the feathers. For a time, all was well. On each visit, the mallard gave one feather to his family. They sold it for sufficient money to support themselves in comfort. However, Bodhisattva's former wife became greedy.

Justifying herself by saying that animals cannot be trusted, she resolved to take by force what the golden bird had been giving her for free. Even though she knew this was her husband, she asked their daughters to help her grab and pluck the bird. The daughters refused, as they were not willing to hurt either their father or a kindly bird, but the former wife went ahead with her greedy plan. The golden mallard was thus plucked and flung into a barrel. His former wife planned to pluck him again when the feathers regrew, and fed him in the meantime. However, she didn't know that if the feathers were taken rather than given, they reverted to simple bird feathers, and when the new ones grew they were also ordinary. The mallard, now plain white, flew away and never came back.

Exactly why Bodhisattva was reincarnated as a bird is unclear, but it was no ordinary bird and served to teach a valuable lesson. Effectively, the recipient of the mallard's goodwill shot the golden goose for not producing eggs faster. Even one golden feather was an unlooked-for bounty and a kind gift; to receive enough to be rescued from poverty should have been more than sufficient. Greed led to the loss of what the family already had and, presumably, a return to hardship.

Half Full or Half Empty?

An alternate take on the question of whether the metaphorical glass is half full or half empty is to realize it does not matter – there is something in the glass, and something is better than nothing. In this tale, the former wife was given enough, wanted more and ended up with nothing. This can apply to situations as well as wealth. There are those who will always focus on the empty part of the glass, and those who will always be grateful for the contents – however small.

Another Avian Incarnation

In another tale, Bodhisattva was reincarnated as a parrot named Radha. He had a brother called Potthapada. Both parrots were captured and sold to a kindly Brahmin, who was very fond of

OPPOSITE: Khmer (Cambodian) Buddhists used decorated silks known as *pidan* as canopies during their religious observances. This example features incidents from the Jataka tales.

BELOW: The paintings of the Mogao cave complex in China were created over hundreds of years. The site is one of several on the Silk Road, which suggests that it was a major artery for the spread of Buddhism.

them. However, although the Brahmin was a good man, his wife was quite the opposite, so the Brahmin told his parrots to watch her while he was away on business.

As predicted, the Brahmin's wife took full advantage of her husband's absence and committed a great many sins. Men visited her night and day, and the parrots observed with disapproval. Eventually, Potthapada decided to speak up, and asked his mistress why she was sinning so lavishly. She reacted badly to being criticized by a parrot, but pretended she was sorry. Picking up the bird as if to pet him, she instead wrung his neck and threw him in the oven.

Radha had advised against speaking up, and now wisely held his peace. When the Brahmin returned, he asked the remaining bird what had happened, but Radha thought it better not to comment directly. He stated that wise people do not say bad things about others – in effect, 'if you have nothing nice to say, say nothing' – and instead mentioned that his brother had been flung into the oven for what he had said. Then he flew away, not desiring to live in that house any longer.

A Learning Experience

It seems that even Buddha needed to learn hard lessons at times, and he was not ashamed to relate tales of his own mistakes if others could learn from them. In one of the Jataka tales, Bodhisattva was incarnated as a jackal. He came upon an unexpected windfall in the form of a dead elephant but could not get his teeth into its tough skin. Eventually, he hit upon the idea of gnawing his way into the carcass by way of its anus.

Tunnelling his way into the carcass, the jackal feasted upon the elephant's innards. This drew him ever further inside until he had carved out a large hollow. He decided to live there, in a house made out of food, and enjoy a life of ease. Eventually, there was little left of the elephant, but by then its skin had shrunk in the sunlight. The jackal could not get out until a rainstorm softened the skin enough to squeeze out – but only at the cost of scraping his fur off. Bodhisattva vowed never to be greedy again, and also to avoid going inside elephant carcasses.

In his final incarnation, the Buddha used this story to remind some of his followers, who were returning to their old ways of greed and craving, of the perils they faced. He did so in a kindly manner, speaking to the whole community rather than singling out those who were backsliding, and using an example of his own former foolishness to soften the lesson. In this case, the only former life identified was that of the Buddha himself.

A Tale of Needless Panic

Many of the Jataka tales feature animals as the protagonists, and often have similarities with fables from other cultures. In some cases, this may be due to cultural exchange, but there may also be an element of parallel evolution. Fables of this sort are based upon the observation of people and animals, the behaviour of whom is surprisingly similar even between cultures that have never met.

At a time when Bodhisattva had been reincarnated as a lion, he lived in a forest with many other animals. Among them was a hare with an overactive imagination and a lamentable lack of courage. One day, the hare was lying in a grove of palm and vilva trees pondering some big metaphysical questions. He was just wondering

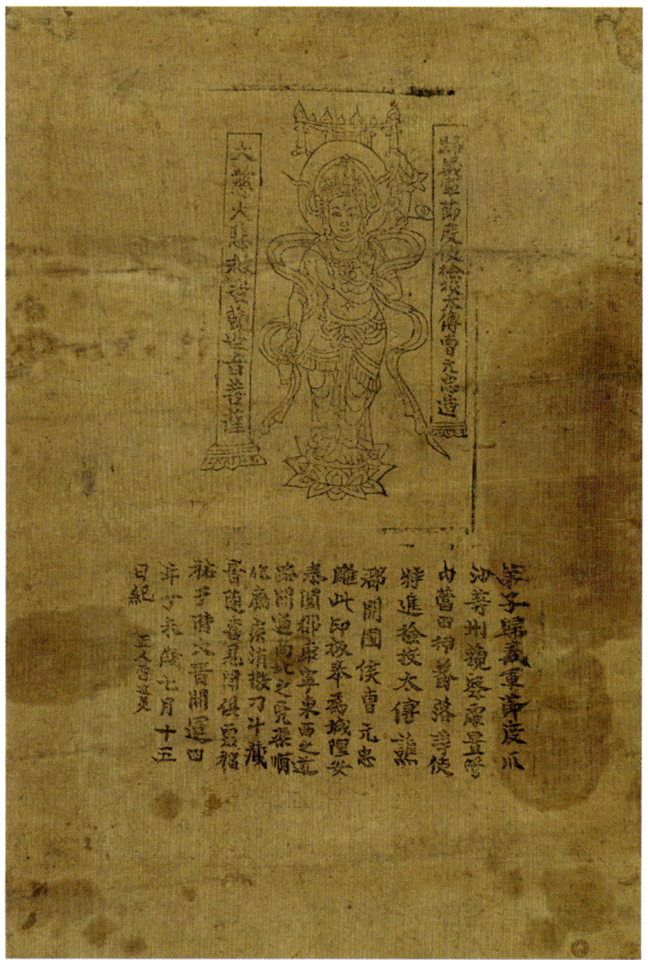

ABOVE: **A depiction of Bodhisattva Guanyin, a Chinese mythological figure based originally on the Bodhisattva Avalokiteśvara, who offers assistance to those in fear or uncertainty.**

what would happen to him if the world was suddenly destroyed, when a vilva fruit fell off the tree. It struck a palm leaf on the way down and made a noise. The hare jumped to the conclusion that the world was ending and made a run for it.

Another hare joined in his flight, asking what had startled him so. At first, the hare would not answer but his companion persisted. At this point, the panicked hare announced that the world was breaking up. Both kept running, and were joined by others. Soon, a great horde of animals was stampeding through the forest. Among them were large creatures: elephants, rhinoceroses and oxen.

Bodhisattva saw the fleeing mob and heard their frightened cries. He knew that the world was not disintegrating and their flight was merely unreasoning panic. However, the animals were endangering themselves by trying to escape from the non-existent threat. Ahead was the sea, and they seemed entirely likely to plunge straight in. Bodhisattva decided to save them, but was aware that halting their headlong flight would take more than calm words.

Running ahead of the mob to the foot of a mountain, Bodhisattva roared loudly, three times. Frightened by this great noise and the sight of a lion in their path, the animals stopped. This permitted Bodhisattva to ask them what they were running from. The nearest animals answered that the world was being destroyed, but Bodhisattva pressed the question. Who had witnessed this event?

The nearest animals thought the elephants would know, but they referred him to the lions. The lions thought the tigers knew, but the tigers thought it was the rhinoceroses. So it went on, with every species sure that some other group knew what was going on, until eventually Bodhisattva asked the deer. They suggested the hares might have some useful information, and eventually they pointed out the original hare. He confirmed that the world was, indeed, in the process of collapsing. At the very moment he was worrying about the destruction of the world he had heard it start, so he must be right.

The lion realized that the hare had jumped to a conclusion upon hearing a fruit hit a palm leaf, but wisely decided to investigate rather than say what he only thought must be true. He offered to go with the hare to the place where the stampede had begun, admonishing the animals to stay exactly where they were. He transported the hare on his back and soon reached the palm grove.

The hare was frightened to go in, so the lion approached the place and found evidence of a fallen fruit. There was no sign of planetary destruction, which confirmed his supposition that the hare had misinterpreted a loud but harmless sound. Returning to the animals, the lion explained what had happened and suggested they go home.

This tale warns of the perils of precipitate action and acting upon imaginary fears. Despite not having seen any evidence that the world was ending, the animals were rushing to their deaths in the very real sea. It is also notable that the panic was self-sustaining and spread as more animals joined in the flight. The tale can be taken as a commentary on the mentality of a mob, with parallels in the modern world.

BELOW: This footed bowl depicts the Jataka tale in which Gauttila, the royal musician, is forced to compete against his own pupil in order to retain his position.

Indeed, in an age of mass communication, this story has never been more apt. Considering where the information came from and how reliable it might be before taking action is always wise. Nor is it desirable to be ruled by phantom fears. A wise person might fact-check before spreading panic.

Failure to Accept Impermanence

Bodhisattva was a kindly and non-violent being, but even he could make mistakes.

On one occasion, he was reincarnated as a humble potter. His would have been a simple but fulfilling life; he had a wife and a family, and made useful items from raw clay. This was obtained from the shores of a nearby lake and river. When a drought dried up the clay, the potter had to venture further afield to gather his raw materials.

At the same time there lived a particular tortoise who was very fond of his home. Like all the other animals, he knew a drought was coming. This would separate the lake from the

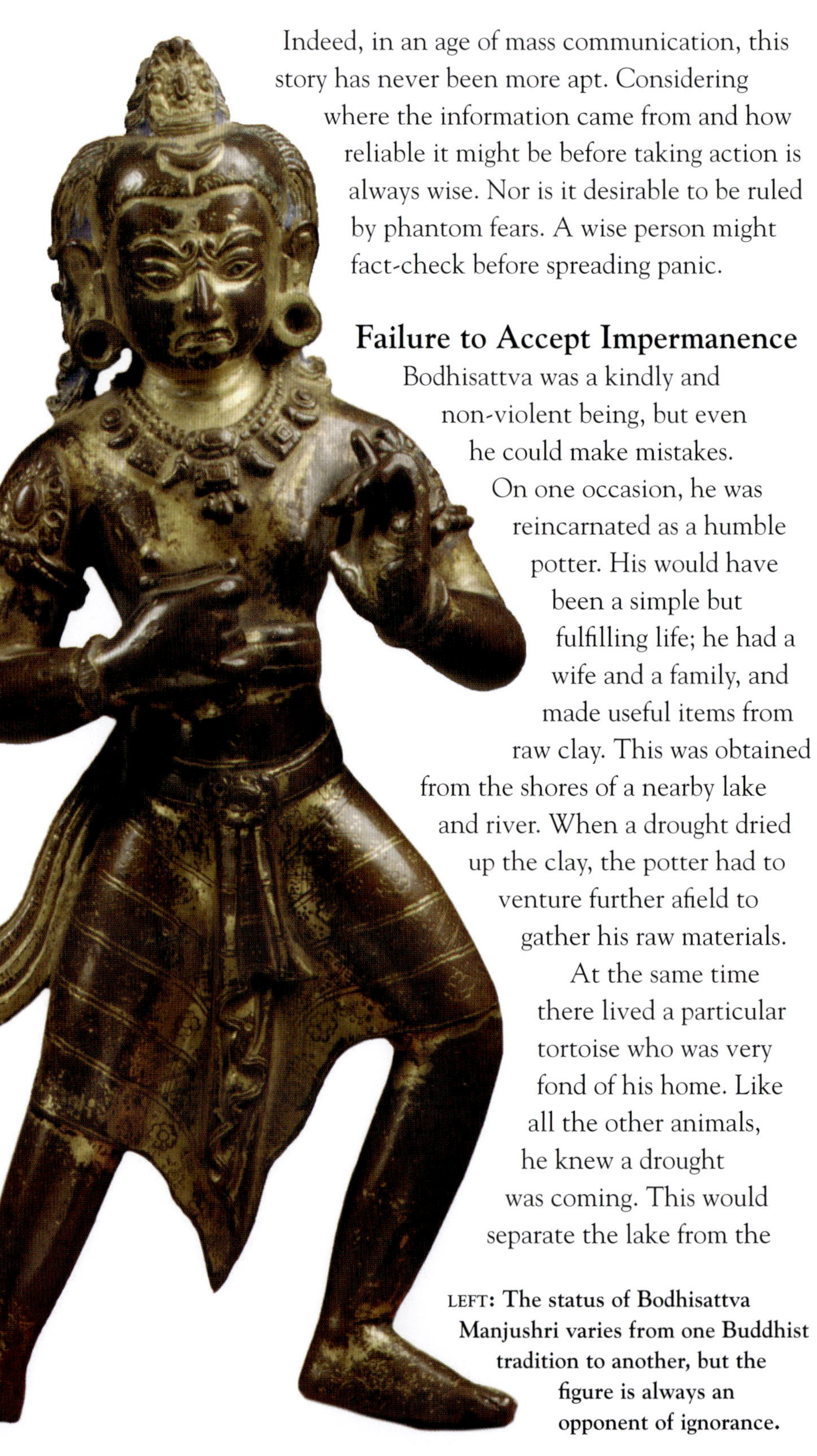

LEFT: The status of Bodhisattva Manjushri varies from one Buddhist tradition to another, but the figure is always an opponent of ignorance.

river that fed it and, while there was still time, most of the creatures moved to the river. The tortoise would not. He loved his home and wanted to stay there. As the drought continued, the lake dried up around the tortoise. To preserve himself until the rains came, the tortoise dug himself into the lakebed mud. Unfortunately, he chose the very spot where the potter intended to collect clay for his work. The potter's spade split open his shell and mortally wounded the tortoise, but he lived long enough to explain his foolishness to Bodhisattva. This in turn he related to the villagers.

The tale, Bodhisattva explained, demonstrated the foolishness of clinging to things that are no longer necessary or useful. Whereas the wiser animals and fishes left their home for a place in which they could survive, the tortoise refused. Where they survived, he died. The villagers were inspired by this wisdom, choosing to let go of impermanent things and to seek what they needed rather than what they wanted.

Letting Go of Cravings

In one of his incarnations, Bodhisattva was a religious advisor to a king, who was widely respected for his virtuous actions. Bodhisattva wanted to know if the respect was earned or due to his important station. To test this, he stole some coins and allowed himself to be caught. The king dealt with him impartially, sentencing him to death despite his high station. Bodhisattva revealed his test and stated that the king really was respected for his deeds rather than his status. He was forgiven and left the palace to become an ascetic.

Along the way, Bodhisattva saw a hawk steal a piece of meat and fly off with it, only to be attacked by other birds. It dropped the food and another bird grabbed it, only to be attacked in turn. He also witnessed a slave invite her lover to visit her. He did not come, and she was saddened but later became resigned to the loss. Bodhisattva realized that life is better when desires are put aside; only then is it possible to be at peace.

Soon afterwards, he encountered an ascetic who was quite happy in his meditation, expecting and craving nothing and therefore satisfied even though he had nothing.

A Cautionary Tale about Perception

In this tale, four sons of the king all wanted to see a Judas tree. Their charioteer was willing to oblige, but could only take them one at a time. The first visited in the spring when the tree was starting to bud; the second saw the tree when it was in full leaf. The third witnessed the tree's blossom while the fourth saw it laden with fruit.

The brothers never thought to compare notes until they were asked about the tree they had seen. Each answered truthfully, creating an apparent contradiction. Puzzled, they asked their

OPPOSITE: The Judas tree is notable for its vibrant pink blossom. It would appear quite different when in bloom from its winter or post-blossom appearance, perhaps confusing unwise young princes, as in the tale.

father why each of them had witnessed something entirely different. Their father replied that it was their fault they did not see the big picture. None of them had thought to ask the charioteer if the tree was always as they saw it.

This tale cautions against assuming that everything is always as it is at that moment, and suggests that someone with wisdom looks beyond the snapshots they experience to see a wider picture of constant change.

The Occasional Wisdom of Women

The Jataka tales concede that wisdom is not merely the province of men, though it seems that recognition of female wisdom is a little grudging at times. One of the Jataka tales concerns a robber named Sattuka whose hitherto successful career came to an abrupt end when he was captured. As Sattuka was being led to his execution, he was spotted by a woman named Sulasa, who fell in love with him at once.

Up to that point, Sulasa had commanded a price of a thousand pieces to spend the night with a man, but she instantly decided that if she could have Sattuka, she would live a respectable life with him. This she secured through bribery, obtaining the release of the robber. The arrangement was mutually satisfactory for a few months and, even though she could have earned a lot of money elsewhere, Sulasa was faithful to her reformed robber.

Sattuka, however, began to long for his old life. He could have left at any time, but instead plotted to kill Sulasa and empty her home of valuables. Sattuka concocted a story about promising a deity who lived on a mountain-top an offering if he were spared, and said that they now needed to go and make it. Naturally, Sulasa must wear all her jewellery to impress the deity.

When they reached the mountain-top, Sattuka told Sulasa of his real intentions. She pleaded with him to be spared, pointing out that she had saved him from certain death and been a good and faithful wife to him. He already had all her riches, and her besides. Sattuka insisted that he was going to kill her anyway. Then Sulasa asked permission to make obeisance before she died, kneeling before Sattuka and touching her head to his foot. She did the same from the sides, and went to kneel behind him.

ABOVE: Buddha is depicted along with some of his female followers on the wall of Borobudur in Java.

This time, there was no obeisance; she pushed her traitorous husband off the mountain-top.

At this, the deity that actually did live on the mountain conceded that women can show wisdom upon occasion. The deity was, of course, Bodhisattva. Sulasa descended from the mountain and went on with her life.

The rather grudging acknowledgement of her cleverness in tricking Sattuka seems a little sexist, but certainly Sulasa's wisdom was rather intermittent. Paying a thousand coins to free a convicted robber then expecting him not to harm her was something of a gamble. This may be another example of craving something to the point where common sense is forgotten. Doing so almost got Sulasa killed, while Sattuka could not be content with the good things he had and met a bad end.

Another Sexist Tale

Although Buddhism came to accept women as monks, attitudes were not always very positive. One tale speaks of a religious advisor to the king who was permitted to ride the king's horse. Everyone admired the animal, and the advisor was pleased. However, when he told his wife about the incident, she told him it was actually the horse's ornamentation the people had admired. If the advisor dressed himself up in the fine saddle and bridle, people would admire him just as much.

Unsurprisingly, this did not go well. Ridiculed for prancing about dressed up as a horse, the advisor angrily returned to confront his wife. She fled, and the king asked his advisor to forgive her and take her back. He stated that women were full of faults so could be forgiven for the occasional nasty prank or piece of terrible advice. His advisor disagreed and married someone else.

This sexist tale was told by Buddha to one of his followers who had come to regret joining the religious community. He was therefore sneaking home to his wife, who provided him with much nicer food than the novice monks got. Buddha explained that the couple were incarnations of those in the tale, and that

BELOW: Whilst Buddha accepted nuns among his followers, the Jataka tales contain several intended to warn male monks about the dangers associated with women.

the monk should relinquish his wife as she had been unkind to him in that previous life.

More on the Evils of Women

In another of the Jatakas, Bodhisattva was a prince who had six brothers. Fearing they would assassinate him, the king sent the brothers into exile with their families. With nothing to eat for days, they began killing and eating one of the women every day until only the Bodhisattva's wife remained alive. At this point, the couple fled from the six brothers, suffering great privations until they reached the Ganges. There, they made a simple home.

One day, the pair spotted a robber floating down the river in a boat. He had been savagely punished; his hands and feet had bee cut off, along with his nose and ears. Nevertheless, they were able to save him and he lived with the couple for a time. Eventually, Bodhisattva's wife fell in love with the robber and decided to get rid of her husband. She pushed him off a cliff and assumed he had died.

RETURNING TO CIVILIZATION, THE FORMER WIFE CARRIED HER ROBBER LOVER AROUND ON HER SHOULDERS AS HE HAD NO FEET, AND PEOPLE GAVE THEM ALMS TO SURVIVE ON.

Returning to civilization, the former wife carried her robber lover around on her shoulders as he had no feet, and people gave them alms to survive on. This went on for years, until they encountered the prince. He had fallen into a fig tree and been rescued by an iguana, and had now returned to take the throne upon his father's death. The prince recognized his traitorous wife and stated that she should die for what she had done. Instead, she was punished by having her lover tied to her back in a basket so that she could never put him down.

This tale was told to convince Buddha's disciples that women are an unwelcome distraction, and are generally bad and unpleasant. This is a theme in various Jataka tales, serving to maintain the values of the community even at the expense of vilifying an entire gender. In this case, one of the monks had fallen in love with a woman he had seen and was unhappy with the religious life. Buddha wanted him to renounce his passion and remain a disciple. As often happened, characters were reincarnations of present friends and enemies. The six brothers were previous incarnations of present disciples and the helpful iguana was Buddha's close friend Ananda. The robber was

Devadatta while the villainous wife was Cinca Manavika, who in a previous life tried to discredit the Bodhisattva.

ABOVE: **Scenes from ten last Jataka stories, hall of Lokahteikpan Temple Pagan, Myanmar.**

Sometimes Violence Solves Problems

In one of the Jataka tales the protagonist is one of Buddha's disciples. In an incarnation as an elephant, he happened across a drunk and belligerent dung beetle. It had consumed some spilled alcohol and fallen asleep in a pile of dung; the dung then collapsed, releasing a powerful odour that offended the passing elephant. It turned away, causing the beetle to think it had frightened the huge beast. The beetle immediately challenged the elephant to a fight, which was accepted. However, rather than its usual weapons, the elephant dumped a huge pile of dung on the beetle and crushed him to death.

Buddha told this story in response to a situation in which one of his disciples beat up a particularly troublesome man who kept pestering the community. The beetle was, of course, a previous incarnation of the pestilential fool, who had a history of making a nuisance of himself across many lives. There is no sign of disapproval for the disciple's actions, and indeed the story relates that the incident had happened before. Perhaps the beetle should have learned his lesson.

BELOW: Buddha's sermons are recorded throughout the Pali Canon. Many are designed to bring the hearer, by a series of small logical steps, to a moment of realization.

A Warning Against the Stupidity of Others

The Jataka tales contain all manner of good advice, much of which concerns a person's own actions. Some are a reminder to be mindful of the possible or likely actions of others. One of them is about an incident witnessed by Bodhisattva as he passed through a small village. The local carpenter was busy and did not want to stop in order to drive away a mosquito that was annoying him. The carpenter asked his son to deal with the insect. For reasons best known to himself, the boy selected a gigantic axe as the ideal implement. He struck a single blow at the mosquito, which had landed on his father's head. The mosquito was entirely obliterated, with the unfortunate side effect of the old man's head being cleavedin two.

Witnessing this, Bodhisattva commented that it was better to have an enemy with sense – who might reasonably be deterred from aggression – than a helpful but stupid friend. Beyond the obvious disadvantages of surrounding oneself with idiots, the tale is a reminder to consider the effects the actions of others might have. If a simple task can be undone by well-meaning stupidity, progress towards enlightenment will surely be impeded by those who think they are helping.

BODHISATTVA COMMENTED THAT IT WAS BETTER TO HAVE AN ENEMY WITH SENSE – WHO MIGHT REASONABLY BE DETERRED FROM AGGRESSION – THAN A HELPFUL BUT STUPID FRIEND.

Devadatta Gets His Comeuppance – Again

In a previous incarnation, Bodhisattva was a mighty elephant who had eighty thousand followers. He was asked by a quail to protect her young, which were in the path of the herd. He did so, guiding his herd around the hatchlings. He warned the quail that a lone elephant was following the herd, over whom he had no control.

The quail asked the lone elephant to spare her children, but this was an incarnation of Devadatta, and instead he delighted in trampling them. The quail vowed revenge, but there was nothing a tiny bird could do to a mighty beast. However, the quail made friends wisely by helping others, and they now teamed up against the evil elephant. A crow pecked out his eyes and a fly laid eggs in the remains so that maggots drove him mad with pain. A frog whom the quail had befriended croaked to lead the elephant in the direction of water, or so he thought.

OPPOSITE: No one could do harm to Buddha. Assassins chose instead to follow him, and he was able to tame enraged beasts just by speaking to them. Even hurled rocks broke apart rather than strike him.

In fact, he was led to the edge of a cliff, and fell to his death. The tale relates just how villainous Devadatta was through his incarnations but also serves as a reminder not to bully those who are weaker, as they may have powerful friends.

Dasaratha Jataka and *Ramayana*

There are close similarities between the tale told in the *Dasaratha Jataka* and the *Ramayana*, one of the great Indian epic poems. Part of the holy writings of the Hindu religion, *Ramayana* is twenty-four thousand verses long and was written down some time between 400 BCE and 100 BCE. The tale itself, and the incidents depicted, are much older.

In *Ramayana*, Prince Rama is the son of King Dasaratha and crown prince of Kosala. He is supplanted and sent into exile, whereupon his wife is abducted by Ravana, the demon-king of Lanka. What follows is an epic tale of adventure and war involving millions-strong armies of apes and the destruction of Lanka before Rama finally returns home.

The *Dasaratha Jataka* makes reference to this tale but is more concerned with spiritual elements. In this version, King Dasaratha had sixteen thousand wives. Bodhisattva was the crown prince but, when his mother died, another of the wives became the main consort and bore the king a son. The king granted her a boon, which she did not at once claim. Years later, she asked that her son rather than Bodhisattva should be crown prince and eventually ruler. At first, he refused, but he was worried that his consort would somehow have Bodhisattva murdered to clear the way for succession. His solution was to send Bodhisattva away until the time came for him to inherit the kingdom.

Bodhisattva was accompanied by his brother and sister, children of the same mother, and left behind his half-brother at the palace. They made a home for themselves in the Himalayas, where they lived a simple life. It had been predicted that the king would live another twelve years after sending away the crown prince, but he died after just nine due to grief at losing his children. His consort ordered that her son be crowned immediately, but the palace officials refused as this had not been the king's wish.

The consort's son went to fetch Bodhisattva and his siblings. They collapsed in grief but Bodhisattva did not. He explained that everything is impermanent and that grief serves no purpose. This caused everyone else to accept the death of the king and

RIGHT: In the Indian epic poem *Ramayana*, the son of King Dasaratha – Prince Rama – is aided by an army of apes in his war against King Ravana of Lanka.

cease to be sad about it. The consort's son then honourably asked Bodhisattva to return to take the throne. He replied that he could not, since he had been sent away for twelve years and only nine had passed. He sent his brother and sister on ahead to

rule in his absence, and they placed Bodhisattva's sandals on the throne rather than using it themselves.

The sandals were apparently good rulers. When Bodhisattva's regents were wrong about something the sandals slapped together to indicate this, and a new decision was made. In this way, the kingdom was governed until the twelve-year exile was over. At that time, Bodhisattva returned home, made his sister his queen and ruled over a golden age lasting sixteen thousand years.

Vessantara Jataka

The five hundred and forty-seventh and last of the Jataka tales is the most famous. In this story, the Bodhisattva was the son of King Sanjaya and Queen Phusati. Both were renowned for their generosity and virtue. Phusati had been the wife of the god Indra in her previous incarnation and had been granted ten wishes. One of them was to bear a son on earth who would be a virtuous ruler. The wish was granted, and during her earthly life, Phusati gave birth to Prince Vessantara, who was an incarnation of Bodhisattva.

ABOVE: The *Vessantara Jataka* is a tale of generosity taken to its utter extreme, in which Prince Vessantara cheerfully gives away everything he can lay his hands on, including his own wife and children.

This was no ordinary child. Moments after being born, he asked his mother for gifts he could pass on to others. Large amounts of money were distributed in his name at that time, and he continued the tradition. Given an extremely valuable necklace by his father, he gifted it to his two hundred and forty nurses. Each time the necklace was replaced, the prince gave it away. He helped a lot of people this way, but there was something unsatisfactory about giving away something that had been gifted to him. He vowed to give anyone anything they asked for, even cutting out his own eyes or heart if someone needed them.

The gods were greatly pleased by Vessantara's generosity, and he excelled in all other ways besides. When he turned sixteen, his parents abdicated and gave him the throne. He married his cousin Maddi and had two children. His son was called Jali and his daughter was Kanhajina. Under Vessantara's rule, the kingdom was happy and prosperous. He made gifts of money to his people every day until they wanted for nothing, after which Vessantara found even more ways to be generous.

The neighbouring kingdom of Kalinga was suffering a drought, which could not be alleviated by their own devout religious observances. Their king therefore sent a party of Brahmins to request assistance, and Vessantara naturally agreed. He had a white elephant that caused nourishing rains to fall wherever it went. Not only did he gift this to the people of Kalinga, but he also sent all its jewelled ornaments and the five hundred attendants who looked after it.

This angered Vessantara's subjects, who feared their time of prosperity would come to an end if he gave away everything of value. They petitioned former king Sanjaya to resume the throne and banish Vessantara, and he reluctantly agreed. Vessantara was given a day to prepare for exile. He suggested that his wife and children should hide their remaining wealth to support themselves, and that Maddi should consider remarrying. However, she would not leave him; Maddi and the children would live in the forest with Vessantara.

The next morning, the family departed, giving away everything they owned as they left the city. The four horses that pulled his chariot were about all that remained to Vessantara, but when a party of Brahmins requested them, he gave them away. Four gods, transformed into deer, came to pull the chariot but more Brahmins asked for them. Their wish was granted, leaving Vessantara and Maddi carrying their children along the road. Such was Vessantara's virtue that the trees lowered their branches so that the weary family could pick fruit. The road was magically shortened, allowing the travellers to reach the city of Ceta in a single day. There,

BELOW: A Chinese bas-relief of the *Vessantara Jataka*, dating from the late sixth to early seventh century.

ABOVE: The *Vessantara Jataka* is one of the most important and popular tales. This scroll illustrating the story is of Thai origin.

Vessantara's uncle welcomed him and offered him the throne. He declined, resting at the city gate rather than entering and moving on in the morning.

Such was the esteem in which he was held that Vessantara was accompanied by sixty thousand nobles of Ceta as he left their city. Again, the road was shortened and they arrived in Vamka in two more days. Indra sent the god Vissakamma to build a home with beautiful gardens for the family. They arrived and moved in, donning the robes of ascetics and living a simple life. In the surrounding forest, even fierce beasts were peaceful. This allowed Maddi to gather fruits without danger.

After a while, an old Brahmin named Jujaka came to see Vessantara with a request. He had a very young and devoted wife named Amittatapana who had attracted the rather nasty jealousy of others. This was because she was such a good wife that others could not match up to her example, and she was saddened by their unkind words when she went to fetch water. Jujaka offered to perform the task instead but she would not let him, suggesting instead that he go to Vessantara and ask to be given a slave.

Jujaka had been to Vessantara's home city but had been driven away. The population resented the fact that their ruler had given everyone what they asked for, and considered those who came with requests to be greedy. However, the gods put Jujaka on the right road, as they approved of Vessantara's generosity, but upon reaching Ceta he fell foul of an ill-tempered pack of dogs. His cries for help attracted a woodsman who had been placed on lookout by Vessantara's uncle in case anyone came seeking him. The woodsman intended to kill the Brahmin in order to protect Vessantara from more greedy people, but the Brahmin claimed to be an ambassador from the king. This meant he could not be harmed, so the woodsman had to let him pass.

Jujaka also deceived the ascetic Accuta, claiming he was simply visiting Vessantara to pay his respects. Thus, he obtained directions for the last part of the journey. He halted short of Vessantara's house and slept in the wilderness so that he could approach when Maddi was away gathering fruits. Maddi realized something was wrong when she had a nightmare about a man in a yellow robe tearing out her heart and her eyes, but Vessantara

ABOVE: Many of the Jataka tales seem strangely familiar when first encountered. Some make reference to Indian mythology or have elements in common whilst others observe human and animal behaviour common across all cultures.

assured her that everything was fine. He knew, of course, that it was not. Indeed, Vessantara knew that Jujaka was coming to ask for his children, so that they might relieve Amittatapana of the task of collecting water and facing the jealousy of others.

Rather than being offended or saddened, Vessantara was pleased; he had not been able to practise generosity for several months and was glad of the chance. He did suggest to Jujaka that he should take the children home to their grandfather in return for a large reward rather than keeping them as slaves, but Jujaka would have none of it. Hearing this, the children ran away and hid. Vessantara went after them and told them he must give them away as part of his progress towards perfection.

Each of the children was assigned a very high price if Jujaka wanted to sell them, after which Vessantara completed the transaction. As the old Brahmin left with his children, Vessantara was at first pleased with his mighty piece of generosity, then saddened at the loss of his family. Knowing that attachment was an impediment in obtaining perfection, however, he duly eradicated his feelings towards his children.

Maddi was unable to return in time to prevent the transaction. Three of the gods blocked her homeward path in the form of a lion, a tiger and a leopard. When she finally reached the house, the children were long gone and Vessantara would not tell her what had happened. She searched all night, and in the morning Vessantara told her what he had done. Knowing that this was an important step on his road to enlightenment, Maddi was pleased.

The god Indra realized that Vessantara would give away his wife if asked to do so, and decided to avoid having her taken by a bad person. He assumed human form and asked to take Maddi. Vessantara hesitated only for a second before agreeing. This supreme act of generosity pleased Indra, who revealed his identity and returned Maddi. He also granted Vessantara eight wishes. Among these was a wish to always have the means to help people and always to do so, to be able to return home and to be reborn in heaven after his death.

BELOW: **In the *Vessantara Jataka*, the Brahmin Jujaka is a self-serving villain. Buddhism places a person's actions far above the status or caste they were born into.**

The children were forced to make a long journey with Jujaka, and he was not kind. He tied them up each night but, while he slept, two deities freed the children and fed them. Meanwhile, they led Jujaka astray and took him to Vessantara's home city instead of his own. There, King Sanjaya was delighted to see his grandchildren. Jali stood by his father's decision to give the children away while

OPPOSITE: Buddha preached a hundred and eight Avadana tales to highlight the effects of one life's deeds on future incarnations. This painted banner illustrates just five of these tales.

Kanhajina decried the cruelty of Jujaka. They were freed by King Sanjaya, who paid the high price Vessantara had set, and Jujaka also received a palace. There, he over-indulged in fine foods and died. Nobody came to his funeral so King Sanjaya took back all he had given to the old Brahmin.

King Sanjaya was saddened to hear how hard life was for Vessantara and Maddi, and decided to bring them home. In addition to fourteen thousand elephants and the same number of chariots, he sent sixty thousand people who had been blessed by Indra and born on the same day as Vessantara. The famous white elephant, returned by the grateful king of Kalinga, also accompanied the party. After a month spent at the forest home with his visitors, Vessantara returned home to be crowned king. Indra sent a rain of jewels so that he would always have something to give away.

During his final incarnation, Bodhisattva revealed that some of the characters in this story were reincarnations of old friends and enemies. The woodsman was Chandaka, the faithful charioteer who took Siddhartha Gautama on his life-changing journeys into the outside world. Jujaka was an incarnation of Devadatta, who betrayed the Buddha and tried to lead the Sangha astray. His family were earlier incarnations of themselves or of close disciples.

Many More Jataka Tales

There are hundreds of Jataka tales, each with a point to make. Many resemble fables or stories told elsewhere while others are entirely unique. One theme running throughout is the appearance of previous incarnations of people who were alive when Buddha told the tale. This suggests that although there is no permanent, unchanging self or soul, a being will continue on the course they are inclined to over many lifetimes, reincarnated in places and in forms that align with their nature. However, it is possible to change this fate at any time through adopting a different lifestyle. The Jataka tales make it clear that those who do not choose to mend their ways are destined to be stuck in a particularly negative cycle of reincarnations until they finally see the light and choose a different course of action.

4

TEACHINGS OF THE BUDDHA

The teachings of the Buddha were not written down until after his death. In order to maintain the purity of the canon, each major segment was recited at a great meeting. This took place several times, right up to the present day.

The oldest known Buddhist writings, dating from the first century, are written on birch bark scrolls. They survived the centuries in a clay pot, that had been buried, though only fragments remain today. The upper part of the scrolls has been lost, but the lower part – which would have been in the centre of the scrolls when rolled up – has partially survived. Other documents of similar or more recent origin have been found, but the majority of Buddhist writings have been copied and recopied down the centuries. As a result, multiple versions of the same story now exist. However, there is a generally

OPPOSITE: The Taima Mandala depicts the western Pure Land of Sukhavati with its associated Buddha, Amitabha. Pure Land Buddhists hope that Amitabha can assist them being reborn in his realm, from where it is much easier to attain enlightenment.

ABOVE: Birch bark was used to record many Buddhist writings. These fragments, although degraded, have survived two thousand years.

accepted body of lore that forms the basis of Buddhist canon and contains the teachings of the Buddha.

Turning the Wheel of Dharma

The wheel, or chakra, is a common symbol of the Dharma, and great teachings are often referred to as a turning of the wheel of Dharma. Each Buddha is said to have turned the wheel three times. In the case of Gautama Buddha, the first turning of the wheel is traditionally held to have taken place in Sarnath, near the confluence of the Ganges and the Varuna rivers. On this occasion, Buddha taught the Four Noble Truths and other important concepts, including the Vinaya that governed the actions of monks.

Buddha's second turning of the wheel is held to have occurred long after his death. In a sermon delivered at Vulture Peak Mountain in Bihar, Buddha taught his followers about emptiness – the concept that everything is devoid of intrinsic value, or a mental state of non-self – and compassion among other subjects. The sermon was kept secret by Nagas until conditions were right for its contents to become known.

The third turning of the wheel occurred when a collection of Sutras emerged during the fourth century, bringing to light additional information that fuelled the emergence of the Vijnanavada or Yogachara school of Buddhism. Various Buddhist traditions place other works within the third turning.

TATHAGATA

Guatama Buddha referred to himself as Tathagata, though the exact meaning of this word is rather vague. A number of definitions exist, but the most commonly accepted is 'one who has thus gone' – essentially, someone who had trodden the path ahead and can show the way. The term is also sometimes used to refer to the potential Buddha found in every person.

The Pali Canon

The Pali Canon is so named because it was written down in Pali. It is also known as Tipitaka, or 'Triple Baskets', in Pali and Tripitaka in Sanskrit. For those following the Theravada form of Buddhism, it represents the whole canon of their religion. Theravada translates as 'Way of the Elders', relating to the fact that this style of Buddhism follows the old ways: the teachings of Buddha, above all else. The Tipitaka is holy to those who follow the Mahayana form of Buddhism, along with later writings recording the teachings of others than the Buddha. Mahayana translates as 'Greater Vehicle' and refers to those who follow the spirit, rather than the letter, of Buddha's teachings.

Initially, there was no written form of the Buddhist canon. When he spoke, Buddha's followers were expected to commit his words to memory. Using human memory rather than some more permanent means to record important information might seem strange, but it avoided certain problems that might arise from committing words to writing. Unscrupulous people might alter or falsify the documents, or else conveniently 'find a repository of hidden knowledge' that presented a version of events to their advantage.

Those who committed the Buddha's words to memory were loyal supporters who were seeking or might even have found enlightenment. They had nothing to gain from changing the Buddha's message and an ethical duty not to do so. They could be trusted to preserve what they heard without being influenced by earthly concerns and to recite it without fear or favour. The mental discipline necessary to retain this knowledge was part of their daily life.

Thus it was that during the Buddha's life there was no need to commit his words to any physical medium. Afterwards, however, his followers decided that they must ensure that the teachings were properly retained and passed on.

BELOW: The largest written work in human history is inscribed on marble slabs at the Kuthodaw Pagoda in Mandalay, Myanmar.

The First Council, as already noted, was convened three months after Buddha died. This was his express wish, and at this council the entire Pali Canon was recited and agreed among those present. While those gifted with a perfect memory, such as Ananda, could be sure they would always get the canon right, for those who were not so far along in their journey this was an opportunity to fact-check.

The First Council was also a momentous occasion for the Sangha, marking the beginning of a new phase. The Buddha was no longer among them to lead and teach; they must decide what to do and how best to go about it. The council might be considered a memorial to the Buddha and his great influence on everyone present, but like all else it would have been viewed dispassionately by those on their way to enlightenment.

According to tradition, the First Council met in 544 BCE but, since there is some debate over the exact dates of the Buddha's life, this is open to interpretation. It was sponsored by King Ajatasattu and was convened in part to address questions of how to proceed further. Some of the monks had chafed under the strictures imposed upon them by the Buddha, and wanted

BELOW: The First Council at Rajagaha represented a 'passing of the torch'. Buddha's disciples were no longer merely followers; they were responsible for preserving and spreading his wisdom.

to soften the rules that governed them or even to do away with them entirely. While it was no great thing for those who had lost faith to go back to their old lives, the teachings of Buddha might become distorted if monks were permitted to do as they pleased.

The council consisted of five hundred monks, all described as Arhats (Arahants in Pali), and therefore living in a state of enlightenment and wisdom. Ananda was told he could be among them if he attained Arhat status in time. Some sources state that he did so; others said that he did not but was granted a special dispensation to attend. Numerous monks made representations for his inclusion as he had achieved a high state of moral and ethical development and had been a trusted companion of the Buddha.

ABOVE: Each Buddha had a personal attendant in addition to chief disciples. In the case of Siddhartha Gautama it was his boyhood friend Ananda, who was blessed with a perfect memory.

Some sources state that Ananda was put on trial during the council, with allegations of various minor transgressions. It is possible that this was part of the process of establishing the correct Vinaya, and certainly by the end of the council there was an agreed set of rules in place. It is said that, in his last days, Buddha told Ananda that after he was gone the Sangha could do away with the lesser and minor rules governing the conduct of members, but did not specify which rules fell into this category. Ananda did not ask, as he was more concerned about the fact that his friend was dying.

distractions, Chandaka realized his error and eventually achieved enlightenment. It may be that this was the intent – his 'punishment' being more of an opportunity to change his ways.

Mahakassapa led the gathering, which first verified that the Vinaya was correctly recalled, by having Upali recite it and the assembled Arahants confirm it. Next was the Dharma, as taught by Buddha. Ananda recited every discourse to the satisfaction of the assembled monks, and the body of teaching was confirmed as correctly recalled. Most of the monks present would not have heard everything the Buddha said, so the First Council was a pivotal moment in world history: the moment when it became possible for all monks to teach the complete Dharma.

Since the First Council, others have been convened. At each, the

THE PALI CANON

The Pali Canon consists of three *pitakas* – 'collections' or 'baskets' – of knowledge. The Vinaya Pitaka is a compilation of the rules governing Buddhist monks, while the Abhidhamma Pitaka is an encyclopaedia of metaphysical concepts. The Suttanta Pitka contains the discourses of the Buddha, by way of which he dispensed his wisdom and taught people about the underlying concepts.

BELOW: The Great Councils ensured that regional versions of the canon – such as they Cambodian example – remained true to the original teachings of the Buddha.

entire Pali Canon was recited, first by an Elder and then by all present. Only when all present agreed that the recitations were correct was the council decreed valid.

The Second Council took place a century after the death of Buddha. It arose out of a dispute over the actions of some monks. Observance of the strict rules governing the Sangha had drifted a little, and some monks believed it was acceptable to eat later than midday, or to eat early then go out asking for food. Mindless repetition of actions or words simply because others had done or said so was another problem, along with using rugs of an improper size. While apparently minor, these and similar transgressions marked a degradation in the purity of religious life, which could place the Dharma in danger of being similarly diluted.

The Second Council

The Second Council was sponsored by King Kalasoka and took place at Vesali. The catalyst was the revelation that some monks were asking for gold and silver as alms despite being forbidden to use those metals, along with other breaches of the Vinaya. A senior monk named Elder Yasa challenged the monks about their behaviour but, rather than being contrite, they offered him money as a bribe. Being above such things, he refused, bringing him into conflict with the greedy monks who tried to have him removed from his leadership role.

BELOW: A representation of the Third Council, convened to deal with important issues that had arisen in the many years since the death of the Buddha.

Elder Yasa sought assistance from more righteous monks, and together they sought the wisdom of the Venerable Revata. The wayward monks also tried to win Revata's support with offers of riches, but were rebuffed. They did manage to win over Revata's assistant, the Venerable Uttara, but his entreaties were not enough to persuade Revata that monks should be dealing in hard currency. He called a council to decide upon the matter. A council of eight Venerables debated the issues and made a ruling, after which the seven hundred monks present recited the canon.

It was agreed that the council had been performed correctly and the questions of monks' behaviour were settled. However, the greedy monks did not accept this ruling and continued in their heretical ways.

BUDDHISM ATTRACTED WEALTHY PATRONS, SO THERE WAS AN INCENTIVE FOR UNSCRUPULOUS PEOPLE TO PRETEND TO BE MONKS IN ORDER TO RECEIVE LAVISH GIFTS.

The Third Council

Heresy continued to be a serious problem after the Second Council. Buddhism attracted wealthy patrons, so there was an incentive for unscrupulous people to pretend to be monks in order to receive lavish gifts. This was bad enough, but these impostors would also teach distorted or simply made-up versions of the Dharma for their own gain and glorification. This could not be permitted to continue, so the Third Council was called in 326 BCE.

The Third Council was sponsored by Emperor Ashoka, a great benefactor of Buddhism. A thousand monks took part, led by Elder Moggaliputta Tissa. He was the author of the Kathavatthu, or 'Points of Controversy', which discusses various questions raised by and about the teachings of the Buddha. Among them is the existence or otherwise of an eternal and unchanging soul.

The primary concern of the Third Council was heresy and the resulting schisms in the Buddhist community. Ironically, it was the support of Emperor Ashoka that fed the worst of the heresies. Originally a patron of many religious groups, the emperor renounced all others and wholeheartedly supported Buddhism. He funded missionaries and the construction of holy sites, pouring his immense wealth into the task. This naturally attracted those who sought to benefit and, although unworthy applicants were refused ordination as monks, many donned the yellow robe and faked it.

The Third Council came about as the result of an incident during which one of Ashoka's ministers ordered righteous monks to include unworthy fakers in their ceremonies. They refused, even when he began beheading anyone who would not obey him. This misguided attempt to impose the emperor's will upon the Sangha came to an abrupt end when the minister found himself facing Ashoka's own brother. He had been ordained and was prepared to die before betraying the principles of the Sangha.

The minister returned to a horrified emperor, who asked for a council in order that they could address the problem by more peaceable means.

After the recitations of the Vinaya and the Dharma, the council addressed the issues of heresy and greed. Emperor Ashoka took part in the questioning of monks from various communities, and those who proved unworthy were expelled. Points raised

OPPOSITE: Emperor Ashoka was a great patron of Buddhism, funding missionaries and building stupas across his realm. His funding also tempted some monks into heresy.

Tibetan Canon

The Tibetan Buddhist canon consists of the Kangyur ('Translation of the Word') and the Tengyur ('Translation of Treatises'), a concept dating from the fourteenth century.

The exact contents of the canon varies over time and between versions. Some texts may be removed and others added as the compiler thinks best. As a result, there is no permanently fixed Tibetan canon.

BELOW: These book covers date from 1410, having been commissioned by the Chinese emperor of the time. They encased a copy of the Tibetan canon.

during the council were recorded, along with their explanation or rebuttal, in the Kathavatthu. A wave of missionaries were sent out after the council had ended, supported by the emperor's resources.

The Fourth Council

Among the lands to which the missionaries went was Sri Lanka, and it was there that the Fourth Council was convened in 29 BCE. This came about as a result of concerns about the purity of the knowledge retained by monks. Many proved unable to remember the entire body of teachings and to recite it correctly. The solution was to create a new body of written works containing the complete and correct knowledge.

The Fourth Council was sponsored by King Vattagamani and involved five hundred monks. Once they had recited the Vinaya and Dharma to the satisfaction of all, they began the work of writing everything down on palm leaves. This represents a shift from relying on devout human memory to a more permanent form of record-keeping, and must have become widespread quite quickly.

The earliest known Buddhist writings were discovered in Afghanistan, very far from Sri Lanka, and may date from the period soon after the Fourth Council. It is probable that they were created later than that, but the earliest find does not

BELOW: The Sixth Council was held in 1954, when Vajiran Gavongs oversaw the daunting task of ensuring all versions of the canon, in all languages, were correct.

necessarily translate to the earliest documents created. Written versions of the Buddhist canon would have been distributed in the years immediately after the council.

Sutras, or Suttas

The Sanskrit word 'Sutra' and the Pali equivalent 'Sutta' can refer to a concise statement or aphorism that encapsulates an important concept or rule. In Buddhism, the term is used to refer to a work of religious doctrine that may be of considerable length. The discourses of the Buddha are presented as Sutras (or Suttas), each with its own points to make and examples to give.

The Modern Councils

For nearly two thousand years, there were no further recognized councils. Gatherings might be called, but none has been given the status accorded to the first four until modern times. The first of these modern councils, the Fifth Council, took place in 1871. It was held in what is now Myanmar under the sponsorship of King Mindon.

The Fifth Council was by far the largest to date, with two thousand four hundred monks led by three Elders. These were supported by a large number of craftsmen, who undertook the inscription of the entire canon on marble blocks. It was followed in 1954 by a gathering of two thousand five hundred monks sponsored by the government of what was then Burma. Whereas the recitation of the Dharma took five months at the Fifth Council, it required two years to complete at this Sixth Council. This was in part due to the presence of monks of many nationalities.

In addition to the usual reaffirmation of the canon, the Sixth Council's task was to ensure that the written versions of the canon were correct in all the languages of those present. Once the impressively few errors had been noted for correction, the way was open for mass publication of the canon in multiple different languages.

The Sutra Pitaka

The Sutra Pitaka, or Sutta Pitaka in Pali, contains the discourses of the Buddha himself, as recited by his followers at the First Council and thereafter. In Sanskrit, the 'Basket of Discourse' is divided into four collections referred to as Agamas, while the Pali version refers to its subdivisions as Nikayas. The contents of both

ABOVE: Little has changed for the modern-day Buddhist monk. Modern vision correction might help with reading the Sutras, but their content remains true to the original teachings.

are broadly the same, but the Theravada branch of Buddhism adds a fifth Nikaya.

The Dirghagama

The 'Long Collection', known as Digha Nikaya in Pali, contains thirty-four Sutras of significant length. The first of these, the Brahmajala Sutra, lays out much of the fundamental doctrine of Buddhism. It begins with a little scene-setting; Buddha was travelling with about five hundred monks, and was followed on the road by Suppiya and his pupil Brahmadatta. They were arguing: Suppiya picking faults with the Buddha's teachings and way of life and Brahmadatta countering his arguments with praise. The Buddha told his followers not to take delight in hearing someone praise him, nor to be annoyed that another spoke disparagingly. Instead, they should concern themselves only with what is right and correct, and ensuring that everyone who wanted to learn could do so.

Buddha followed with a short discourse on how people should live, following his example. They should be compassionate and care about the welfare of every living thing. They should be chaste and honest, truthful and trustworthy. A good person should eschew malicious speech and gossip, and indeed should only speak when there is something useful to say.

Further, a follower of the Buddha should not indulge in pointless pleasures and fripperies. Dancing and music are merely distractions, while perfumes and ornaments are unnecessary. Followers should refrain from accepting gold and silver, or slaves, or raw meat and grains. They should not try to own land or livestock and must not engage in commerce or errand-running.

BELOW: The vitarka mudra gesture symbolizes deliberation or discussion, indicating that this representation of Buddha is engaged in teaching or preaching a sermon.

These strictures would set the Buddha's followers apart from the lay folk who might run a farm, marry or trade in the marketplace as part of their daily lives. Yet, without such ordinary folk to support them with alms, the monks would not be able to live. Some of the Buddha's rules are therefore applicable to wider society. He forbade corruption, deceit and trading using altered weights and measures, along with various forms of violence and robbery.

After this short section on morality, there follows a longer one, which repeats earlier material in more detail. This section rather pointedly compares the strict abstention of Gautama Buddha with the looser standards of 'some ascetics and Brahmins'. This section decries the practice of demeaning those who are wrong or misinformed, instead showing how Gautama Buddha does not delight in showing someone they are wrong, restricting himself instead to quietly showing them what is right. Nor does he take orders from or try to please Brahmins and kings by running errands for them or otherwise doing what they want.

This is further expanded upon by a third section on morality, which goes into even more detail. Adherents are warned against making a profit or even just a living from false arts, such as divination, by various means. This was a source of income and power for well-established religious figures, who would be approached for their advice before military campaigns and other large projects. Gautama Buddha warned against being drawn into such activities, regardless of the gains to be made.

ABOVE: When documents were copied and recopied, the original illustrations might or might not be updated to reflect current culture. This segment of a Sutra has been dated to 797.

Next, the Brahmajala Sutra lists all manner of ways to be wrong, and warns against them. This section is specific about the number of variants concerning a given area of error. There are eighteen ways to put forward incorrect theories about the past, and four ways to be wrong about the existence of an eternal soul or self. These are each enunciated and dispelled in turn. After this, attention turns to the forty-four ways of being wrong regarding theories about the future.

The Brahmajala Sutra states that these sixty-six views of the past and the future are all that are available, and all are wrong. The reasons for being wrong vary; some are due to ignorance or a lack of knowledge in critical areas. Others are the result of cravings or mistaken beliefs thought to be knowledge.

The Ambattha Sutra

The Brahmajala Sutra is followed by the Ambattha Sutra, which is largely a social commentary. Gautama Buddha did not approve of the caste system in place at the time, nor of the many ways of the Brahmins who were at the top of it. The Ambattha Sutra is named for Ambattha, a pupil of the Brahmin Pokkharasati, who was rather full of himself.

Ambattha was sent by his master to find out if the Buddha really did possess great wisdom. In order to test him, despite the respect shown to him by the Buddha, Ambattha was rude, walking up and down while speaking, even though the Buddha was seated. When challenged about his behaviour, Ambattha said that he did not need to show respect to an inferior. Buddha chided him about his ego and pointed out that Ambattha had come seeking answers but would not pay respect to the one he hoped would give them.

Ambattha responded by cursing Buddha and his clan, claiming they failed to show respect to Brahmins, highest of the four castes of the time. In return, Buddha pointed out that Ambattha's clan was actually of lower status than his own due to their bloodline. This angered Ambattha's attendants, but Buddha shut them down by suggesting they should speak on Ambattha's behalf only if they thought he was unable to stand up for himself. They next turned on Ambattha when he admitted his inferior bloodline. Buddha then defended Ambattha, explaining that his ancestor was a mighty sage despite an inferior bloodline.

By a clever set of examples referring to various circumstances caste members could find themselves in, Buddha brought Ambattha to the understanding that respect was not a simple matter of caste membership. He taught that to stand highly in the spiritual realm a person must cast aside notions of caste or race along with ego and pride, and must do more than simply memorize the holy lore. Someone who uses knowledge to act the part is a fraud and a charlatan, and not worthy of the respect that should be due to a true sage.

Pokkharasati was furious with his pupil for the disrespect he had shown to Buddha and went to apologize. Having ascertained for himself that Gautama Buddha really was a great man, Pokkharasati invited Buddha to eat with him. At this meal, Buddha delivered a discourse on generosity and morality, among

BELOW: The cover of a copy of the Ashtasahasrika Prajnaparamita Sutra, depicting the goddess Prajnaparamita along with two Bodhisattvas. Events from the life of Buddha flank the central illustration.

other subjects. This inspired Pokkharasati to become a lay member of the Sangha; no longer a rich and powerful Brahmin, he was content to be an ordinary follower of Buddha.

The Mahanidana Sutra

The Mahanidana Sutra is often referred to as the 'Great Discourse on Causation'. It begins with Ananda announcing that he fully understands the concept of dependent co-arising. While

BELOW: A fresco from Wat Chiang Mun in Thailand, depicting the Buddha and some of his followers in the forest. Groves and parks were common gifts by powerful rulers to the religious community.

this can be simply stated to be a relationship between cause and effect, observer and observed, and so forth, it is rather more complex than Ananda thinks. Buddha tells him so.

Buddha pointed out that lack of understanding of the Dharma is what causes the current generation to be so confused and thus trapped in the cycle of rebirth. He then gave several examples, beginning with ageing and death. Buddha stated that if anyone asked if there is a reason for ageing and death, the answer is yes. If they ask what the reason is, the answer is that ageing and death are the inevitable result of birth. He then explained the cause of birth as becoming, and that becoming is the result of clinging. In this part of his discourse, Buddha laid out the chain of causes leading back to consciousness. Consciousness results from name-and-form. Thus, by experiencing the cosmos, a person becomes tied into a chain of cause and effect leading to birth and, ultimately, death.

Buddha then expanded on each concept in turn, beginning by bringing Ananda to the understanding that if there was no birth there would be no ageing and death in any realm – humans, Devas or animals. He worked through the whole of the Law of Twelve Causes, which is discussed in Chapter 1. Some causes can have more than one effect. Buddha gave the example of

RIGHT: Having accumulated sufficient virtue and wisdom, Buddha seated himself beneath the Bodhi tree and let it all fall into place. This was the final, overdue, unlocking of his enlightened status.

how craving can lead to quarrels and fights, as well as being part of the chain leading ultimately to ageing and death.

The discourse then turned to the concept of self. Buddha began by explaining the various ways a person can delineate a self in terms of form or formlessness, a finite existence or an infinite one, and when the self has these attributes – now, or at some point in the past or future. Someone who does not delineate a self does not become obsessed with these attributes or the need to attain them at some point in the future. Buddha explained that the self is not defined by what the person feels or experiences, and warns against assumptions about what constitutes the self. Everything that is felt is dependent upon conditions and perception, and is inconstant. Basing the assumption of a self upon feelings is to become entangled in transitory experiences. The Mahanidana Sutra also lays out how consciousness works for different kinds of being, and how it is possible to transcend the limitations of perception to achieve higher states of consciousness.

The Mahaparinibbana Sutra

The Mahaparinibbana Sutra, or 'Discourse on the Great Final Extinction' is the longest of the long discourses, and contains a great deal of material that is dealt with in greater detail in other

Sutras. It tells of the death of the Buddha and its effects on the Sangha. This came as no surprise; Buddha knew he was coming to the end of his life and announced a few months beforehand that he would be dying soon.

In the months preceding the death of Buddha, many of his disciples came to see him. Others also sought his wisdom, among them the minister of King Ajatasattu of Magadha. He told Gautama Buddha that his king had decided to make war on the Vajjis, and wanted to know how well this would turn out. Buddha questioned Ananda on the state of the Vajji people and learned that they were still practising the Dharma they had been taught. Hearing many good things about them, he informed the minister that so long as the Vajjis continued these practices they would be invulnerable to King Ajatasattu's assault.

In addition to relating the events that occurred, this tale is a rather broad hint that those nations that follow the Dharma will prosper and be safe, and those that do not will suffer. Next, Buddha turned his attention to the *bhikkus*, or monks. He laid out the conditions under which they would prosper. This was similar guidance to that given to nations: if the monks continued to live their good lives and observe the Dharma, they would not decline.

Buddha and his followers travelled for a while after this, and along the way he expounded many truths. The Mahaparinibbana Sutra is in many ways a summary and reminder of the Buddha's

PARINIRVANA

Parinirvana, or Parinibbana in Pali, means 'nirvana after death', in other words the moment an enlightened person leaves the cycle of death and rebirth. This was the moment Buddha had been working towards for many lifetimes, albeit deliberately delaying it so that he could first assist others in achieving the same goal.

BELOW: An account of the parinirvana of Buddha. This was the culmination of many lifetimes' work and a reward for his long efforts.

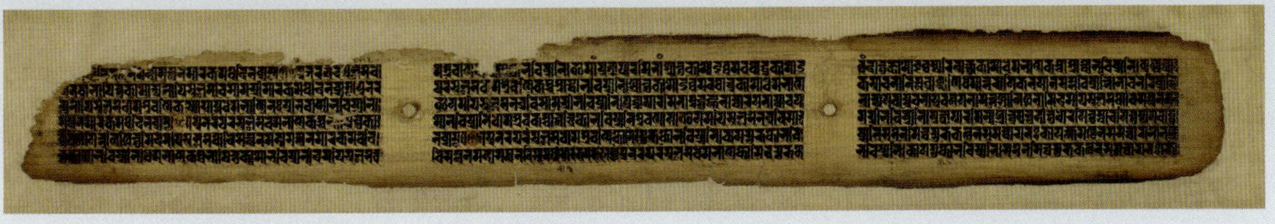

ABOVE: Avalokiteshvara is a manifestation of the transcendent Buddha Amitabha. His task is to protect the world and the Dharma until the next Buddha arises.

teachings, delivered in narrative form during his final journey. Eventually, he came to Kusinara, and spoke with his closest disciples for the last time. Admonishing them to abide always by the Dharma, he told his disciples not to grieve; when he departed, he entered a state of meditation, rising swiftly through the *jhanas*, and passed away from the mortal world.

The Mahaparinibbana Sutra records that despite Buddha's request that they did not grieve, Devas and *bhikkus* alike mourned his passing. earthquakes and thunder shook the world, and those monks who had not yet completely freed themselves from passion were overcome with emotion. Those who were more enlightened accepted the situation; Buddha's teachings had prepared them to accept the impermanence of all things – even Buddha himself.

The mortal remains of Buddha were honoured for several days before being cremated. Everything but his bones burned away, whereupon a rain fell from the heavens to extinguish the funeral pyre. The relics of the Buddha were distributed in eight parts, and over each a stupa was erected in his honour. Similarly, stupas were built over his ashes and even the funeral urn, and the Buddha was honoured in many places.

The Madhyamagama

The Madhyamagama, or Majjhima Nikaya, translates as 'Medium-length Collection'. It contains one hundred and fifty-two Sutras dealing with many aspects of Buddhist life. Some of these Sutras are attributed to specific disciples.

THE ITIVUTTAKA, OR 'THUS-SAIDS' TAKES ITS NAME FROM THE INTRODUCTION TO EACH OF ITS SHORT SUTRAS – 'THUS IT WAS SAID BY BUDDHA.'

The Samyuktagama

The Samyuktagama, or Samyutta Nikaya, translates as 'Cluster Collection'. It contains some seven thousand seven hundred and sixty-two Sutras arranged by topic. Among them is an account of the Buddha's first sermon, delivered to the five ascetics who had been his companions before enlightenment. This work contains the fundamental concepts of Buddhism: the Four Noble Truths and the Eightfold Path.

The Ekottarikagama

The Ekottarikagama, or Anguttara Nikaya in Pali, translates as 'Item-More Collection' and is a collection of short Sutras dealing with various topics. The first group refers to single concepts or topics such as the Buddha; the second group is in pairs. This progresses up to eleven topics. It is arranged this way as an aid to memory, allowing a practitioner to learn and remember a great deal of specific knowledge.

The Khuddaka Nikaya

The Khuddaka Nikaya is found in the Pali Canon but not in Sanskrit versions of the canon. Its name refers to 'lesser' or 'small' books, of which there are fifteen, or eighteen in the Burmese version. The collection begins with the Khuddakapatha, or 'Short Passages' containing basic concepts of Buddhism. Next is the Dhammapada, or 'Path of Dharma', which provides guidance for living within the Dharma. Udama, or 'Exclamations', contains parables and stories.

The Itivuttaka, or 'Thus-saids' takes its name from the introduction to each of its short Sutras – 'Thus it was said by Buddha.' Each Sutra deals with a single topic relating to the Dharma. The Sutta Nipata, or 'Sutra Collection', contains seventy-one slightly longer Sutras dealing with important

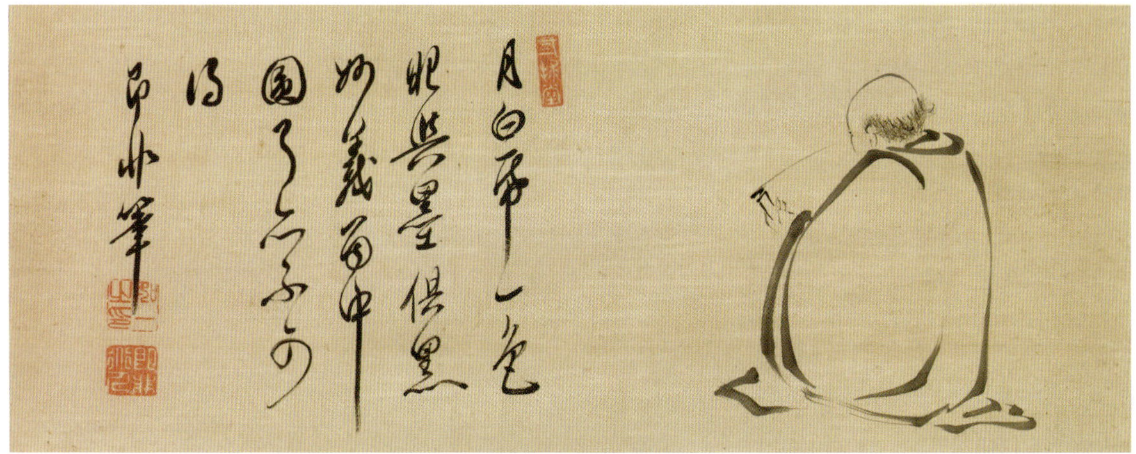

ABOVE: In the early 1600s, a Chinese monk named Yinyuan Lonqui arrived in Japan and began to spread what would become known as Zen Buddhism, along with other Chinese cultural influences.

concepts, such as ceasing to cling to earthly things. This is followed by the eighty-three poems of the Vimanavatthu ('Stories of Celestial Mansions'), which relate to how various deities came to be reborn in their heavens. The Petavatthu ('Stories of the Hungry Ghosts') deals with the opposite: how bad people came to be reborn in this unpleasant form.

The Theragatha and Therigatha ('Verses of the Elder Monks' and 'Verses of the Elder Nuns') contain poems telling of the early monks and nuns. Their difficulties are described, along with how they came to enlightenment. The former lives of the Buddha are next recounted in the five hundred and forty-seven Jataka tales.

The eleventh book of the Khuddaka Nikaya is Niddesa ('Exposition') and takes the form of commentaries on various other parts of the canon. It is followed by further analysis in Patisambhidamagga, or 'Path of Discrimination', which answers key questions about the Buddha's teachings.

Apadana ('Stories') contains biographies of the Buddha and forty-one Paccekabuddhas – 'solitary' Buddhas who achieved enlightenment without assistance and did not remain in the world to teach – as well as five hundred and eighty-nine enlightened monks and nuns.

It is followed by Buddhavamsa, the 'History of the Buddhas', and then by the Cariyapitaka or 'Basket of Conduct'. This work contains stories about the Buddha's previous lives that illustrate certain aspects of his teachings, notably the 'perfections' a Buddha must achieve.

The remaining three books are unique to the Burmese version. Nettippakarana and Petakopadesa deal with aspects of Buddhist doctrine, while Milindapanha ('Questions of Milinda') is in dialogue form, as an Arhat monk answers the questions of King Milinda and converts him to Buddhism.

The Lotus Sutra

The Lotus Sutra is a text in the Mahayana tradition that is particularly popular in Japan and China. It describes the Buddha sitting on Vulture Peak Mountain, delivering a sermon to a vast audience. From a point between his eyes, Buddha sent forth a ray of light that illuminates all the thousands of worlds from the hell realms to the heavens. Buddha stated that those who remain in the world to teach others are superior to those who seek only their own enlightenment.

Buddha then explained that previously he had taught only a part of the Dharma, since the true scope of his full teachings might intimidate some listeners. He revealed that the path of the Arhat is available to everyone and he can show them the way. Those who choose not to follow the way are doomed to be reborn in a hell and then as humans suffering all manner of discomforts.

The Lotus Sutra contains a number of parables that serve as an illustration of its contents, along with tales from the very distant past when the Lotus Sutra was taught in other aeons. In it, Buddha reveals that in fact he achieved Buddhahood countless aeons ago and that his well-known life as Siddhartha Gautama

BELOW: The Lotus Sutra contains some spectacular revelations about the nature of the universe and the lives of the Buddha. Buddha stated that he had reserved these teachings at first as they were too much for most people to comprehend.

RIGHT: The Lotus Sutra speaks of Bodhisattva Perceiver of all the World's Sounds, often shortened to 'Universal Gateway'. It states that this Bodhisattva will hear cries for help from anywhere and provides protection against fear, swords, demons and all manner of other perils.

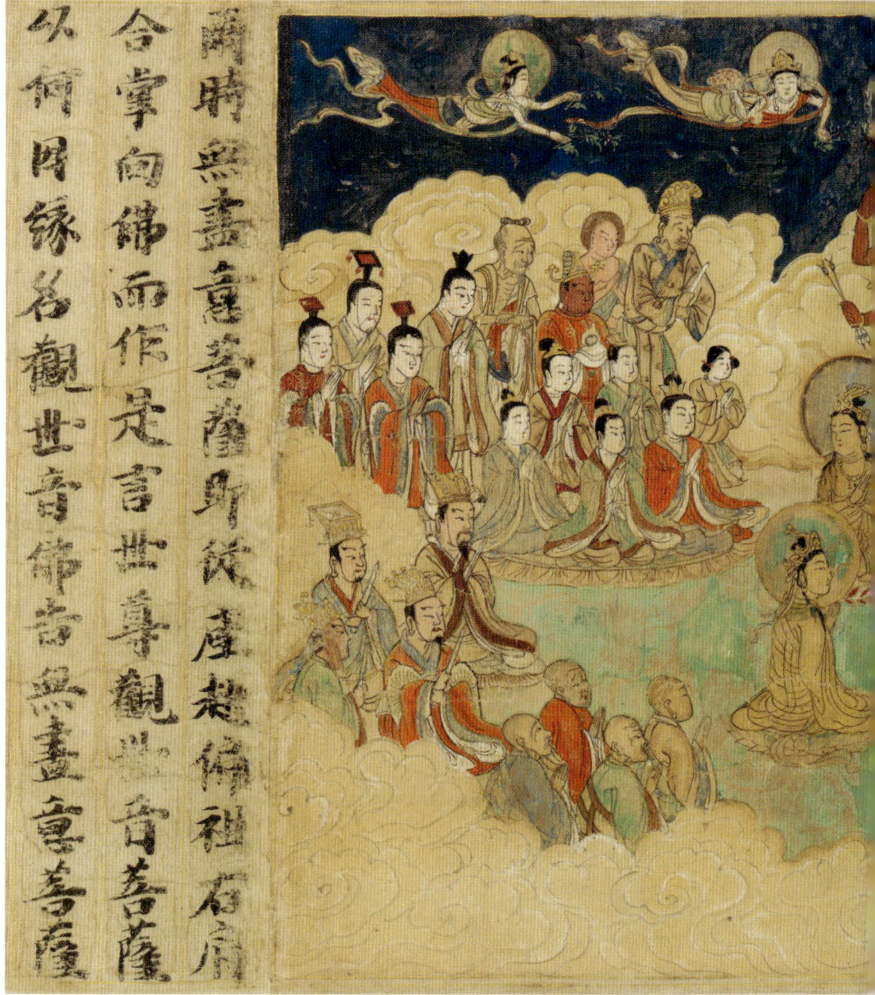

was an act, intended to demonstrate the path to Buddhahood and to inspire others to follow it.

The Avatamsaka Sutra

The Avatamsaka Sutra, or 'Flower Ornament Sutra', is an important part of the Mahayana canon. It is popular in both Tibet and in East Asia. It is probable that it was compiled over a long period, starting around five hundred years after the death of Buddha. The Sutra contains information on a variety of subjects, notably the ten stages through which a Bodhisattva must progress towards Buddhahood.

Key concepts are often repeated throughout the canon, and the Avatamsaka Sutra is no exception. It covers subjects such as

the central Truths of Buddhism, but it is narrative rather than prescriptive for the most part. An idea of the variety and scale of Buddhism is presented through the journey of Sudhana as he encounters fifty-three Bodhisattvas of varying social status. He is eventually able to perceive the cosmos as a vast network of interconnected phenomena.

Buddhism and Sex

In most schools of Buddhism, the stance on sex is simple and clear-cut for monks and nuns – it is completely forbidden. This is not always the case, however. Some schools, notably in Japan, permit priests to marry. For lay people, the basic rule is 'do not engage in sexual misconduct', which is open to interpretation.

BELOW: In some Buddhist traditions, Vajradhara is a primordial Buddha who personifies the whole body of teachings and is the ultimate source of Tantric Buddhist texts.

There is no absolute rule on the subject: no list of sins or prohibited activities that is the same from place to place. Lay Buddhists must make their own decisions on the subject, though some lines are easily drawn. Some forms of sexual activity, such as non-consensual sex, are harmful to the victim and therefore obviously immoral.

Beyond this point, much depends on personal views and local attitudes. Buddhism generally considers sex between people who love one another to be a positive thing, but this does not necessarily relate to sex within marriage always being positive. It is the relationship that matters, not the legal status. Most Buddhist traditions do not make distinctions based upon gender, though Tibetan Buddhism differs in this regard. Tantric sex makes use of meditative techniques, or it might be said that some forms of meditative technique make use of sex. There is a common misconception that the word 'Tantric' always has sexual connotations. This is not the case. The word simply refers to any activity following the principles of the Tantras: documents detailing a variety of practices involving mantras, meditation and the principles of Yoga.

Yoga

The practice of Yoga dates to long before the creation of the Yoga Sutras by the sage Patanjali around 400 CE. Before this, techniques were taught directly and preserved by human memory. Yoga is not simple to define, but a useful working definition is that it is intended to create a strong link between mind, body and spirit through breathing and meditation. There are purely physical benefits, and indeed to many modern people this is the primary or only focus. However, there is a difference between 'doing Yoga' in the same mindset as attending an exercise class and practising Yoga as a means of spiritual development.

YOGA IS NOT SIMPLE TO DEFINE, BUT A USEFUL WORKING DEFINITION IS THAT IT IS INTENDED TO CREATE A STRONG LINK BETWEEN MIND, BODY AND SPIRIT THROUGH BREATHING AND MEDITATION.

The one hundred and ninety-six Yoga Sutras teach how and why to perform Yoga, leading to its deeper purpose of reducing the suffering experienced in life. The extreme practices of ascetics, which unlocked their psychic abilities, are not appealing to most people but may represent the earlier forms of Yoga that were codified by Patanjali. Buddha and his followers were well aware of these concepts and would have made use of them in their own meditations.

Non-violence

The teachings of the Buddha contain occasional examples of violence done when necessary. This is an unfortunate fact of life in an imperfect world. However, to progress towards enlightenment, it is necessary to not want to do harm to anyone or anything. A Buddhist lifestyle leads naturally to non-violence in any case. Most violence arises from negative emotions or cravings and, since Buddhists are taught to rise above such things, they will have fewer reasons to cause harm.

The Buddha was most definitely a peaceful person, who tried to live in harmony with the people and creatures around him. This does not translate to advocating universal pacifism, however. Pacifism is the refusal to commit violence under any circumstances, a philosophy only workable when someone else is willing to protect the pacifist society against those who would do it harm. A community of monks can be pacifists if there are soldiers willing to protect them from harm, which raises the question of whether those whose profession revolves around violence can be considered good people.

If it is necessary to kill or injure someone to stop them harming another, then this act stems from a desire to protect

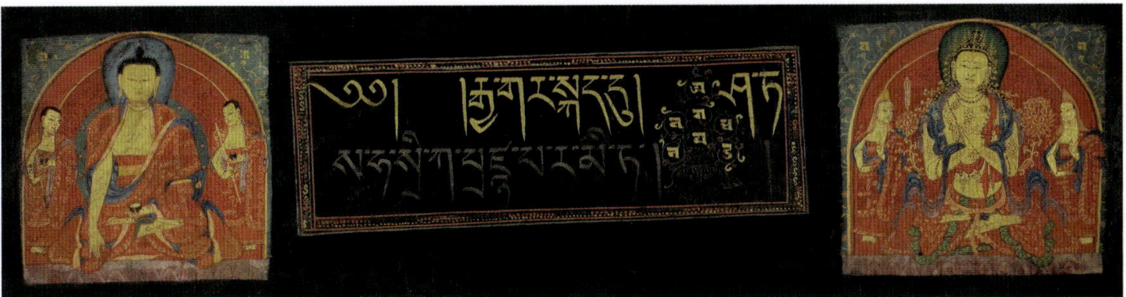

ABOVE: A page from the Astasahasrika Prajnaparamita Sutra, or 'Perfection of Wisdom' Sutra, dating from the sixteenth century.

rather than hatred or anger. It is therefore acceptable, though incompatible with enlightenment. Committing necessary violence does not preclude someone from trying to progress towards enlightenment, but every act of course generates Karma. A soldier or a ruler may have to take actions that harm others in order to discharge their responsibilities and to protect others, and this can be considered righteous if their motives are positive. They cannot be a monk and still fulfil their role, and they cannot fulfil their role and be a monk – but if violence truly is necessary then it is not contrary to the Dharma.

A Vast Body of Teaching

In his lifetime, Gautama Buddha taught on a great many subjects. It may be that some of his discourses were spontaneous, such as the occasion when a monk dissuaded a persistent nuisance with blows. Buddha then told a story about how a similar incident had occurred between them in a previous life. Other discourses resulted from interactions with his followers or visitors, taking the form of answering questions or addressing concerns. There were also lengthy sermons on a number of important subjects.

However, not all of the Buddha's teaching came in the form of words. It is one thing to deliver a speech or create a rule, and entirely another to live it. The Buddha taught many of his lessons by living them. He begged for food on the streets of a city his father ruled; he left behind his worldly possessions and never tried to make himself more comfortable by acquiring more. His own family members were treated no differently to other monks. In this, Gautama Buddha led as well as taught, and can fairly be said to have 'shown the way' rather than merely telling people what path they should follow.

OPPOSITE: The god Vajrabhairava is a rather fearsome representation of enlightenment before whom ignorance and self-interest flee in terror. He is considered to be the vanquisher of death since he frees mortals from the cycle of death and rebirth and thus the dominion of Yama.

5

DIVINE AND EXTRAORDINARY BEINGS

Buddhism recognizes a great many supernatural beings and creatures. Some of them are deities or beings found in Indian mythology while others are previous incarnations of Siddhartha Gautama. Other Buddhas are also acknowledged and are venerated to a greater or lesser degree depending on location.

The Buddha is definitely an extraordinary being, but that does not translate to being divine or supernatural in the sense of a god or demon. Siddhartha Gautama was a man who lived and died, though he did achieve something truly special in his lifetime. He was also an incarnation of a being who had gained virtue over many lifetimes and was not the same as the typical person. At times, that being had existed as a god or some other kind of powerful being, including sages with Yogic powers. Yet, Siddhartha Gautama did not retain these powers in his earthly life.

OPPOSITE: Amoghasiddhi Buddha is one of the five Dhyani-Buddhas. He is associated with the colour green and the wind, and he personifies the accomplishment of all intentions.

The Laughing Buddha

For many Westerners, the image that leaps to mind when Buddha is mentioned is a fat, laughing figure. This might seem strange, given that Buddhism is opposed to the sort of over-indulgence that leads to obesity. Good humour is perfectly all right, but a Buddha who eats too much might not be following his own laws.

In fact, the 'Laughing Buddha' is a representation of a Chinese monk named Budai, who is thought to have lived in the early 900s. As a protector of children and bringer of prosperity, he seems a generally good fellow, and it has been suggested that he is associated with Maitreya, the next Buddha. Some traditions recognize him as a Buddha while others might say that the 'Laughing Buddha' is an icon of Western pop culture rather than of real religion.

BELOW: Despite its iconic status in Western culture, the 'Laughing Buddha' is contentious. Some traditions hold that he is a manifestation of the next Buddha, Maitreya.

These apparent contradictions are reconciled by the Buddha's own teachings. There is no immutable self or soul; if there were, the Siddhartha Gautama might have retained the powers wielded by previous incarnations. Instead, those powers belonged to the current incarnation and were left behind at rebirth. The being that eventually became the Buddha changed over many lifetimes, though virtue was retained from one life to the next. Thus, the previous incarnations of the being who became Buddha were not Buddha but were on their way to becoming Buddha.

The word 'Bodhisattva' is often used to refer to the previous incarnations of Siddhartha Gautama as he lived many lives and gained in virtue, and some use the word only in this context. Others, notably those following the Mahayana branch of Buddhism, refer to anyone who has set out to achieve enlightenment as a Bodhisattva. Some of these people are sufficiently advanced that they have great wisdom or even magical powers, while others are humble but devout aspirants who have far to go.

There are also multiple Buddhas who have appeared throughout history or who are destined to do so. To be accorded Buddha status in Theravada Buddhism, a person must have achieved enlightenment by their own efforts. Those who are guided can be enlightened but they are not Buddhas.

The Previous Buddhas

Buddhist writings recognize a variable number of Buddhas. Some sources state that there are a thousand Buddhas in every *kalpa* (aeon), others that that an incalculable number of Buddhas have existed in previous *kalpas* and cycles of the universe. Not all *kalpas* have a Buddha. Those that do not are referred to as 'dark *kalpas*'.

Twenty-eight Buddhas are named in the Pali Canon, along with one who is yet to come. Their stories vary but each achieved enlightenment by their own efforts and came to it after making a Great Departure from their home and meditating under a tree. The trigger for this process was the Four Signs – an old man, a sick man, someone who had died and an ascetic. The identity of the trees where enlightenment was achieved are recorded along with the Buddha's name, family and their closest disciples.

BELOW: The temple at Wat Suthat in Thailand is surrounded by twenty-eight pagodas, each of which represents a different Buddha.

OPPOSITE: A panel from a portable shrine depicting the descent of Buddha from the Trāyastriṃa heaven at the summit of Mount Meru.

The earliest documents of the Pali Canon do not list all these Buddhas. Seven, known as the Buddhas of Antiquity, are named. Three of these – Vipassi, Sikhi and Vessabhu – lived at the end of the previous aeon, the *vyuhakalpa*. Kakusandha is the first Buddha of the present aeon, the *bhadrakalpa*. He is followed by Konagamana and Kassapa, with Gautama Buddha the fourth of the aeon.

Buddhavamsa, or 'History of the Buddhas', is a later addition to the Pali Canon. It describes each of the Buddhas encountered by Bodhisattva in his previous lives, plus Gautama Buddha himself and Maitreya, the future Buddha-to-come. Of these twenty-nine Buddhas, five have existed or will exist within the current *kalpa*, with the others arising in earlier aeons. This tradition is followed by Theravada Buddhists, primarily in South East Asia and Sri Lanka, while in Tibet and eastern Asia it is commonly acknowledged that vast numbers of Buddhas have existed throughout the aeons.

The Buddhavamsa follows the same format for most of the known Buddhas. Their lives are generally very similar. Each is born into a rich or powerful family and lives in a palace with many beautiful women for a time before leaving to seek enlightenment. Each has their own great accomplishments before and after they 'turn the wheel of Dharma'. Each holds three great assemblies and presides over three 'penetrations', where the Buddha's teachings get through to those who hear them and bring them to a state of wisdom. These penetrations and assemblies generally specify enormous numbers of people, in some cases many times more than the hundred and twenty (or so) billion humans estimated by scientists to have ever lived.

Unknown Buddhas

Some Buddhas are unknown to history and tradition. They are known as Pratyekabuddha in Sanskrit and Paccekabuddha in Pali. These are individuals who achieved a state of enlightenment without assistance but did not remain in the world as teachers. Had they done so, they might have attracted followers and left behind a legacy. Instead, they quietly left the cycle of samsara and made no mark upon the world.

Becoming a Buddha

The requirements to become a Buddha vary between sources. Sanskrit and Tibetan sources generally agree that there are twelve actions that all

Buddhas have in common. This is not a checklist of acts to be carried out so much as an observation of key points in the existence of all Buddhas. Pali documents differ, but state that there are thirty achievements that are obligatory for all Buddhas.

Some of the acts common to all Buddhas are impossible to achieve by a conscious choice made within their lifetime. Therefore, a potential Buddha must lay the groundwork in previous lives, setting in motion a chain of events that will lead to their birth as a possible Buddha-to-be. They must then fulfil the requirements for emergence. These are clearly stated but at the same time imprecise. For example, it is clear that a Buddha must define good and evil acts, but exactly what this means can be unclear. A potential Buddha must be born into the Tavatimsa heaven in the life before the one in which he attains

BELOW: The Twin Miracle, wherein Buddha emitted both fire and water from his body, demonstrated his primacy over rival religious teachers. This miracle is a required act for all Buddhas.

Buddhahood, and will both inspire others to become a Buddha and predict someone achieving that status. A Buddha must live at least three-quarters of his expected lifespan and must convert a suitably large number of people, including his parents. He must appoint two chief disciples from among his followers and instruct the people in how to discern good and evil deeds.

Sanskrit documents state that a Buddha must also hold a great assembly of his followers at Lake Anavatapta, from which the four great rivers of Jambudvipa flow, and perform the Twin Miracle. The Twin Miracle is sometimes known as the Miracle at Savatthi, since this is where Gautama Buddha performed it for the second time. The first occasion was at his home town, Kapilavatthu. On the second and more famous occasion at Savatthi, Gautama Buddha was engaged in a debate with rival religious leaders. They performed several impressive miracles, but Buddha shut them down with his own spectacle. Emitting fire from his shoulders and water from his feet, he manipulated both, then expanded their scope to light up the whole cosmos.

THE TWIN MIRACLE IS SOMETIMES KNOWN AS THE MIRACLE AT SAVATTHI, SINCE THIS IS WHERE GAUTAMA BUDDHA PERFORMED IT FOR THE SECOND TIME.

Multiple images of the Buddha appeared, and he began debating the Dharma with his own image. Rain fell, but as on some other occasions, it wet only those who wanted it; everyone else stayed dry. A huge wind blew away the pavilion of the rival teachers, and then the teachers themselves. Most of them committed suicide, so great was their shame. Around ninety thousand people were converted upon witnessing this feat. Buddha then ascended into the Tavatimsa heaven to teach Dharma to his mother. After three months, he returned, accompanied by the gods Indra and Brahma.

The Tibetan version of this tradition differs in some details. It specifies that the potential Buddha must be an accomplished individual with many skills, and must live in a palace before his Great Departure to seek enlightenment. Notably, Tibetan tradition includes a requirement to defeat the evil Deva Mara.

In Mahayana Buddhism, the concept of Trikaya ('three bodies') applies to Buddhas. These are the *nirmanakaya*, or 'body of transformation', which is the earthly form of the Buddha; the *sambhogakaya* ('body of enjoyment'), which exists in heaven; and the *dharmakaya* ('body of essence'), which is the formless state of unmanifested, limitless knowledge.

Buddhas of the Pali Canon

The earliest Buddha named in the Pali Canon is Tanhankara Buddha, who was the first Buddha of the Saramanda *kalpa*. He achieved enlightenment under the ruk-aththana tree and was followed by Medhankara Buddha then Sarankara Buddha. Little is known about the first three Buddhas, other than a brief reference. After them came Dipankara Buddha. He was the last to be born in that *kalpa*, and was the one who predicted the coming of Gautama Buddha.

BELOW: Some traditions state that there are a thousand Buddhas in each *kalpa*. If so, then Dipankara Buddha was the thousandth of his aeon. However, we only know of four of them.

Dipankara Buddha was the son of King Arcishtra. He chose this family while residing in the Tusita heaven awaiting his next rebirth, and entered the womb of Arcishtra's wife Susila. She gave birth during a visit to the lotus tank, upon an island that magically sprang up on it. Upon the birth of Dipankara ('light bearer'), a great number of bright lamps appeared, giving Dipankara his name.

After living in a palace with many beautiful women, Dipankara encountered his Four Signs and left to become an ascetic. He achieved enlightenment under a pipal tree and demonstrated his wisdom in debate with other religious teachers.

His fame was such that a man named Sumedha, who was the current incarnation of Bodhisattva, came to see him. Sumedha had hoped to bring a lotus flower as a gift, but the king had acquired them all for the same purpose. Instead, Bodhisattva was given some lotus flowers by a girl. Sumedha then approached Dipankara Buddha respectfully and presented his gift. Dipankara then revealed that Sumedha would some day be reborn as Siddhartha Gautama and become a Buddha. He also named the two chief disciples and attendant who would accompany him in that lifetime.

This is a feature of all Buddhas – they must predict the emergence of another – but in the case of Dipankara, his prediction was particularly important. It was in this lifetime that Sumedha realized he could achieve enlightenment and chose to do so slowly in order to help others, rather than seeking his own nirvana by the fastest route possible.

Kondanna Buddha was the son of King Rammavati and his wife Sujata. As with the other Buddhas, it is said that he was amazingly tall – 28 cubits, or over 12 m (39 ft). He had three palaces – again, this is a common feature of the historical Buddhas – in which he lived for ten thousand years with many beautiful women. When it was time, he left home in a chariot and practised austerities for ten months before attaining enlightenment. Like the other Buddhas, he held three great assemblies of followers, whose numbers are spectacularly huge. In the case of Kondanna Buddha, it is said that his first sermon was heard by ten crores of monks. A crore is ten million, giving a total of a hundred million people at this gathering.

ABOVE: When Sumedha met Dipankara, the Buddha of his day, Sumedha lay down in the road so that Dipankara would not have to muddy his feet. Dipankara Buddha recognized the virtue and humility that would someday lead Sumedha to Buddha status.

The stated numbers of people to whom the Buddhas preached are always vast, and exceed the total population of earth through all of its history. This can be interpreted in a variety of ways, as can statements that Buddhas lived incredibly long lives. Both Hindu and Buddhist mythology have a tradition of using enormous and specific numbers to convey an impression. Whether or not these figures are meant to be taken literally or

OPPOSITE: Some of the Buddhas made their Great Departure in a chariot or on horseback. Others rode elephants. The Great Departure is another required act in the life of a Buddha.

are a literary device is an open question. Perhaps the answer is a phrase found at the beginning of many documents, such as the discourses of the Buddha: 'Thus have I heard'.

The followers of Kondanna Buddha were provided with food by a nobleman named Vijitavin, who later gifted his kingdom as well. This was one of Gautama Buddha's incarnations, in which he gained virtue by good deeds. Dipankara predicted this particular Bodhisattva would one day be Gautama Buddha, and named his chief disciples.

Mangala Buddha was the son of a senior member of the Kshatriya (warrior) caste, named Uttara, and is said to have shone with greater glory than other Buddhas. He lived for nine thousand years in his palaces before departing on horseback to seek enlightenment. After eight months of austerities, he achieved his goal, and thereafter the aura emanating from him could be seen across all the worlds. Mangala Buddha is recorded as standing 80 cubits (over 36 m) high and living for ninety thousand years. He preached three great sermons and was honoured by Bodhisattva, who gave his entire fortune to the Buddha of the day.

Sumana Buddha also lived for ninety thousand years and was also a member of the Kshatriya caste. Sumana made his Great Departure on an elephant, taking ten months to achieve enlightenment. He gave three great sermons, of which the last was attended by the god Sakra and Atula, a Naga king who performed music and gave great gifts. Sumana Buddha predicted that Atula would some day become a Buddha, inspiring him to greater efforts to achieve this goal.

Revata Buddha lived for six thousand years as a member of the Kshatriya caste before departing in his chariot to seek enlightenment, which he attained under a naga tree after seven months of austerities. At his second gathering, he taught King Arindama, and it is said that a trillion people and Devas came to hear his third great sermon. It is not possible to know how many came to the first; their numbers were beyond calculation. Revata Buddha predicted that the Bodhisattva of the day, a man named Atideva, would become a Buddha after Bodhisattva gave Revata his cloak.

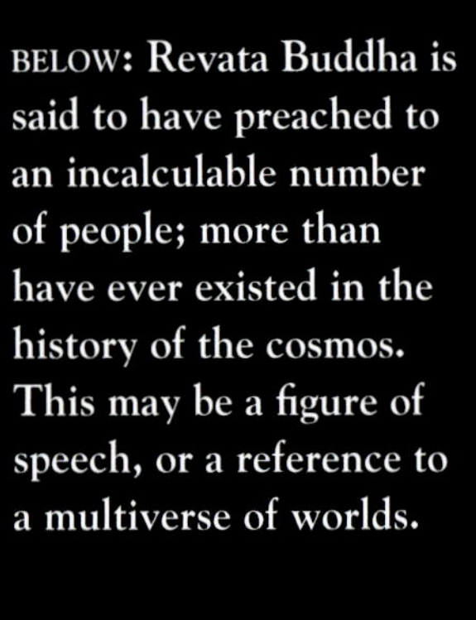

BELOW: Revata Buddha is said to have preached to an incalculable number of people; more than have ever existed in the history of the cosmos. This may be a figure of speech, or a reference to a multiverse of worlds.

Sobhita Buddha is also said to have attracted an incalculable number of people to his first gathering, though the figure of a trillion Arhats is also mentioned. He was a Kshatriya, son of Sudhamma and born in the city of that name. After nine thousand years spent living in his three palaces, Sobhita Buddha achieved enlightenment after just seven days of austerities. He lived for ninety thousand years. At the time, Bodhisattva was incarnated as a Brahmin named Sujata. He gave charity to the Sobhita Buddha, who predicted Sujata would some day become a Buddha.

Anomadassi Buddha was said to be able to bring enlightenment to anyone who heard him speak. He prepared for the life in which he became a Buddha over sixteen periods, each of a thousand *kalpas*, before being reborn in the Tusita heaven. From there, he chose King Yasava and his wife Yasodhara to be his parents. Upon his birth, there was a rain of jewels, and thereafter he lived for ten thousand years in his palaces. Anomadassi Buddha achieved enlightenment after ten months of austerities. He preached the usual three great sermons and performed the

Twin Miracle, converting kings from Soreyya and Radhavati. During his one hundred thousand years of life, he encountered Bodhisattva in the form of a Yaksha chief. The term Yaksha is at times loosely used to refer to beings with a supernatural nature, which can include powerful gods or even Buddhas, but more specifically to describe a supernatural being of lesser status than a Deva. Some are helpful to humans, some malevolent, but all possess great power. There is also a small ethnic group of this name, creating the potential for further confusion.

Paduma Buddha encountered Bodhisattva when he was incarnated as a lion, which gave due reverence to Paduma and was recognized as a future Buddha. Paduma Buddha is described as 58 cubits (over 26 m) tall, and one hundred thousand years old at the time of his death. His Great Departure was aboard a chariot, after which he required eight months to achieve enlightenment.

Narada Buddha was a crown prince who gave up his kingdom to seek enlightenment under a sona tree. His wisdom defeated the king of Mahadona, a Naga who would destroy any part of his city in which the people were disobedient or would not pay their taxes. Narada Buddha converted the Naga, ending his reign of terror, and soon afterwards received gifts from Verocana, another Naga king.

Padumuttara Buddha lived for ten thousand years in his palaces, with forty-three thousand beautiful women. After seeing his Four Signs, he attained enlightenment in seven days. He encountered Bodhisattva in his incarnation as Jatila, a regional official, and recognized his future Buddhahood. It was during this time that many of Buddha's close associates conceived of their desire to become enlightened, embarking on a path that over many lives would lead to their final incarnation as his companions.

Sumedha Buddha spend nine thousand years in his palaces, with forty-eight thousand women, before making his Great Departure on the back of an elephant. After half a month, he achieved enlightenment under a nipa tree. The Bodhisattva of the day was Uttara, a young Brahmin who gave his great wealth to Sumedha Buddha.

Sujata Buddha lived for nine thousand years in his palaces before setting out on horseback to seek enlightenment. After

ABOVE: Each Buddha lived for a very long time in three splendid palaces. Having more to give up than the average person was a factor in becoming a Buddha.

nine months, he achieved it under a velu tree. He encountered the Bodhisattva of the day in his incarnation as the ruler of four continents, who also had magical powers. Bodhisattva gave his entire realm to Sujata Buddha along with great treasures and lesser gifts, and was named as a future Buddha.

Piyadassin Buddha encountered opposition in the form of Sudassana, a Deva king who was spreading incorrect information. This was successfully countered with a teaching of the Dharma to vast numbers of people. Prince Mahapaduma of Kumudanagara

sent an elephant named Donamukha to kill Piyadassin Buddha, but it was deterred with a few words of his wisdom. The Bodhisattva of this time was a Brahmin named Kassapa. He built a park for Piyadassin Buddha and his followers, and was pronounced a future Buddha.

Atthadassin was born in the city of Sobhana, and lived for ten thousand years in his palaces before departing on horseback. Enlightenment required eight months of austerities, after which he is said to have shone with an immeasurable amount of light for 20 km (12.5 miles) above and below where he stood. The Bodhisattva of his day was Susina, who was an ascetic. Atthadassin Buddha lived for a hundred thousand years.

Dhammadassin Buddha, like others, is said to have shone with light and dispelled darkness. He is credited with preaching the Dharma to immense masses of people, with gatherings numbering in the billions, including humans and Devas. The god Sakra attended Dhammadassin Buddha's third gathering and played pleasing music. He was honoured with the prediction that he was a future Buddha.

Siddhattha Buddha should not be confused with Siddhartha Gautama, who became Gautama Buddha. Like many of the Buddhas of antiquity, he shares a name with someone from Gautama Buddha's time. His life followed the usual pattern: ten thousand years living in the palaces with forty-eight thousand beautiful women, followed by a Great Departure. Siddhattha Buddha searched for enlightenment for ten months before

OPPOSITE: Kakusandha Buddha is one of the seven Buddhas of antiquity, and the first Buddha of our present *kalpa*. He is said to have lived for forty thousand years.

finding it under a kanikara tree. The Bodhisattva of his day was named Mangala, and was honoured for bringing gifts of fruit.

Tissa Buddha lived for seven thousand years in his palaces before making his Great Departure on horseback. He practised austerities for eight months before attaining enlightenment under an asana tree. Tissa Buddha is said to have been 60 cubits (over 27 m) tall, and lived for a hundred thousand years.

Phussa Buddha lived for nine thousand years before leaving his home riding an elephant. He achieved enlightenment after six months of austerities and encountered Bodhisattva in his incarnation as a warrior-nobleman named Vijitavin.

Vipassin Buddha is credited with enlightening an incalculable number of followers. He shone with a radiance that could be seen for 91 km (56.5 miles). Vipassin was gifted with a golden seat inlaid with jewels by the Naga king, Atula. Atula possessed great psychic powers and was recognized as a future Buddha.

Sikhin Buddha's aura was rather more modest, but still visible for 37 km (23 miles). He was given gifts by the Bodhisattva of the day, a warrior-noble named Arindama. These included food and drink, ten million robes for the Buddha's followers and a riding elephant.

Vessabhu Buddha lived for six thousand years in his palaces, with thirty thousand beautiful women, before setting forth in a golden palanquin to seek enlightenment. He achieved it after six months of austerities and lived for another sixty thousand

BELOW: Each Buddha would 'turn the wheel of Dharma' three times in his lifetime with great sermons that would have profound effects on huge numbers of people.

years. The Bodhisattva of his time was Sudassana, a warrior, who gave gifts of food and clothing.

Kakusandha Buddha made his Great Departure in a chariot, striving for eight months before attaining enlightenment under a sirisa tree. The Bodhisattva of his day was a warrior named Khema, who gave gifts of ointment, wild liquorice, cloth and bowls to the monks.

Konagamana Buddha is recorded as only having one great gathering, though he achieved three 'penetrations' – occasions upon which he brought a great many people to enlightenment. His Great Departure was made on the back of an elephant. The Bodhisattva of his day was Pabbata, a warrior, who gave gifts of sandals and cloth, including Chinese silk.

Kassapa Buddha was a Brahmin who gave up his riches and performed great acts of charity towards the poor. He lived in his palaces for two thousand years before achieving enlightenment after seven days of striving. The Bodhisattva of his day was Jotipala, a Brahmin. Kassapa Buddha was the last before Gautama Buddha, the 'current' Buddha. Maitreya Buddha will emerge at some point in the future, and will be the fifth Buddha of this *kalpa*.

OPPOSITE: Konagamana Buddha is one of the seven Buddhas of antiquity, emerging after Kakusandha Buddha. Their careers are detailed in the Buddhavamsa.

The Dhyani-Buddhas

Mahayana Buddhism holds that the Dhyani-Buddhas are 'self-born', celestial beings who have existed from the beginning of time. They are sometimes referred to as 'Meditation Buddhas', 'Transcendent Buddhas' or 'Wisdom Buddhas'. There are five, each associated with a particular colour, direction, sense and other characteristics. According to some sources, the Dhyani-Buddhas have manifested on earth as one of the Buddhas. In some traditions, one of their number is given leadership status over the others, or a sixth Dhyani-Buddha is recognized.

Deaths and Relics

The Buddhas of antiquity are variously referred to as having 'waned' or 'burned out', indicating that the light they brought to the cosmos finally came to an end. In most cases, this was after incredibly long lifespans in which they converted enormous numbers of people. After their deaths, the relics of the Buddhas were taken away and holy structures – stupas – were constructed to house them. Sources also record the constructions of monuments to the departed Buddhas, usually of a staggering size that is unlikely to be a literal measurement.

Each of these stupas at the great temple complex of Borobudur contains a representation of one of the Dhyani-Buddhas.

In Pure Land Buddhism, it is held that a monk named Dharmakara made a series of vows before setting out to attain enlightenment. One of these vows was to assist anyone who followed him in attaining their own enlightenment. He is known as Amitabha Buddha. By devoting themselves to him, adherents hope to be reborn in Sukhavati, the Pure Land, for their next life. It is much easier to attain enlightenment in the Pure Land, making this route attractive to those who feel they are not capable of taking the more usual path.

BELOW: One of the Dhyani-Buddhas makes the bodhyagri mudra, or 'wisdom fist' gesture. This identifies the figure as Vairocana Buddha.

Amitabha Buddha is popular in China and Japan as the guide to the Pure Land, but in Tibet and Nepal, this style of Buddhism is less prevalent and he is revered as one of the Dhyani-Buddhas. His earthly manifestations are as Gautama Buddha and the Bodhisattva Avalokiteshvara. The latter is a popular figure, revered for his resolve to bring every person on earth to enlightenment before attaining his own nirvana.

Amitabha Buddha has water as his element, red as his colour and the begging bowl as his symbol. His mount is the peacock and his direction is west. He is associated with the sense of taste, and therefore with the tongue. His position within the human body is in the mouth. Some sects in Japan consider the other four Dhyani-Buddhas to be manifestations of Amitabha while others consider Amitabha and the others to be manifestations of Vairocana.

Vairocana Buddha is sometimes considered to be one of the Dhyani-Buddhas, and sometimes not. Many of those who do count him among their number consider Vairocana to be the foremost of them. He is associated with the colour white and the sense of hearing. His symbol is the chakra, or wheel, and his mount is a dragon or lion.

Amoghasiddhi Buddha is associated with the colour green and the north. He is sometimes known as the Lord of Karma, and is empowered with all-accomplishing wisdom. He is capable of converting envy and all the negativity that arises from it into positive ambition, and can calm anxiety.

Akshobhya Buddha is associated with the east and the colour blue. He is renowned for his patience, having vowed never to become angry. He has the ability to discern between what is real or true, and what is unreal or false. Meanwhile, Ratnasambhava Buddha is associated with the south and the colour yellow, and is renowned for his generosity. He is often depicted holding a magical jewel that can grant wishes, or a begging bowl.

Some Buddhist traditions recognize an Adi-Buddha, a first or primordial Buddha who came into being before all else in the cosmos. From him, by way of five kinds of wisdom and five meditations, came the five Dhyani-Buddhas. In this tradition, neither the Dhyani-Buddhas nor the Adi-Buddha ever came to the mortal world. The Adi-Buddha is often identified with

Beings That Are Not Devas

Certain kinds of being share some characteristics with the Devas but are not the same. Among these are the Bodhisattvas. These Buddhas-to-be are certainly above the normal run of humanity and may be incarnated one or more times as a Deva, but it is their nature as Bodhisattvas that is important rather than their current Deva status. For example, the next Buddha, Maitreya, is currently in the Trāyastriṃa heaven and is a Deva there, but he will be a human in the next life and ultimately a Buddha.

In Tibetan Buddhism, a Yidam is a deity that embodies the meditative goals of an individual. Some of these are gods, some are Buddhas, others are notable figures deemed worthy or appropriate. They do not play the role of Devas in the usual sense, even if the being is itself a Deva. A Yidam is better thought of as a personification, guide or focus for meditation.

RIGHT: **Vajra Yogini is a meditation guide, helping those with strong emotions or desires channel them into more enlightened directions. She also shows how mundane daily experiences are part of the path to enlightenment.**

Vajradhara, whose symbols are the thunderbolt and the bell. He receives the vows of defeated spirits, who must pledge they will no longer inhibit the work of Buddhists. Beyond this, he is too occupied with larger concerns to intervene on earth but works through the god Vajrasattva.

Devas

The term Deva is found in both Buddhist and Hindu mythology, and can loosely be translated as 'deity' or 'divine being'. However, the gods of Buddhism are not as all-powerful as those of most other mythologies. They are neither responsible for the creation of the world nor for major processes, such as the destruction of the cosmos at the end of an aeon. Nor are they immortal. Devas may live a long time compared to mortals but they are born and die – and are reborn – according to the same rules.

BELOW: Carvings at the Shwe Indien stupa in Myanmar depict a Buddha surrounded by Devas, reflecting their role as guardians of the world and the Dharma.

ABOVE: **A relief from the Borobudur temple complex, depicting dissolute and disreputable behaviour. Even Devas were prone at times to negative traits such as these.**

Devas are people, albeit powerful ones, and have their own personalities and goals. Many are flawed, displaying character traits considered negative, such as pride or jealousy. Some will intervene in earthly affairs, but rarely in a dramatic manner. Buddhist Devas are more likely to speak words of wisdom or guidance to someone than to hurl thunderbolts. Most are highly knowledgeable but lack insight in some key areas. For example, a Deva may not know that there are higher worlds than the one they inhabit.

Devas are invisible to normal humans, but those who have developed the correct psychic power can see them. This is termed the *divyacaksus*, or 'Divine Eye'. Likewise, they cannot be heard except by those who have developed a psychic form of hearing. A Deva can, of course, choose to manifest and be seen by all. When they do, the more powerful of them are observed to shine with an inner radiance. They can also fly rapidly over great distances by their own will, whereas the lesser Devas typically require some form of magical transport, such as a flying chariot or a mount of some kind.

Most importantly, Devas are not objects of worship. They are respected for their power and wisdom, but they are no more to be worshipped than a human king or wise ascetic. Devas lack the ability to escape from the cycle of samsara or to show another how to do it, and are thus a part of the cosmos rather than its rulers.

There are multiple kinds of Deva, some of which are very different from one another. Those of the formless realm (Arupyadhatu) do not interact with the rest of the cosmos. They have no physical form and spend their time in meditation. It is possible to become a Deva of this kind by powerful meditation in a previous lifetime.

THE DEVAS OF THE PLEASURE-REALM (KAMADHATU) ARE THE CLOSEST TO MORTALS IN THEIR CHARACTERISTICS. THEY HAVE A PHYSICAL FORM, WHICH IS TYPICALLY LARGER THAN A HUMAN, AND IN SOME CASES INDULGE IN SIMILAR PLEASURES.

Devas of the form-realm (Rupadhatu) do have a physical form but one that is different from that of mortals. They have no gender and do not feel emotions. The lowest of them are the Brahma Devas, who have attained the first level of *jhana*. They have the most contact with the mortal world of all the form-realm Devas. Above them are the Abhasvara Devas, the Subhakrtsna Devas and the Brhatphala Devas, who have attained the second, third and fourth *jhanas* respectively. They are increasingly distanced from the mortal realm. Above these are the Śuddhāvāsa Devas, who are reincarnations of those who died having almost achieved enlightenment. After a lifetime protecting Buddhism on earth, these Devas become enlightened and leave the cycle of samsara.

The Devas of the pleasure-realm (Kamadhatu) are the closest to mortals in their characteristics. They have a physical form, which is typically larger than that of a human, and in some cases indulge in similar pleasures. This can be a distraction that ultimately results in rebirth in the mortal world. The lower Devas of Kamadhatu dwell on the slopes of Mount Meru.

The Catummaharajika Devas

The lowest of the Deva worlds is Catummaharajika, which is named for the Four Heavenly Kings who dwell there. Each has a retinue of semi-divine creatures, which can be minor Devas, and is responsible for a segment of the world. These Devas are guardians of the Buddha, and according to some sources, they protect all his followers as well. They are also responsible for ensuring records are kept of all meetings among Devas, and send out messengers into the world to see if mortals are behaving righteously. This takes place on the eighth day of each lunar half-month. On the fourteenth day, the great kings send their sons out on the same mission, and the day after that they personally manifest in the mortal world.

Vaisravana is associated with the north and is the leader of the Four Heavenly Kings. In addition to generally protecting Buddhism, he is particularly concerned with upholding the Vinaya – the rules governing the life and conduct of monks. He is known by other names, including Jambhala and Kubera.

BELOW: Vaisravana is the leader of the Four Heavenly Kings, and is particularly concerned with protecting the rules by which Buddhist monks live their lives.

Non-Immortal Gods

Like the other Devas, the Four Heavenly Kings are not immortal. Some sources give their lifespans as ninety thousand years. When this time is up they are reborn into a new life, possibly in an entirely different world. Someone else will then be reborn with this godly identity.

The latter is the name of a Hindu god, with whom Vaisravana shares many characteristics. This is common in Buddhism, but the Buddhist version of a given god may differ considerably from the Hindu tradition. Vaisravana's entourage consists of supernatural beings called Yaksas.

As a guardian of the Buddha and his followers, Vaisravana gifted the monks with sacred chants to ward off rogue supernatural creatures that might do them harm. His breath is dangerous, so Vaisravana covers his mouth to protect those he comes into contact with. His epithet is 'Hearer of Many Teachings'.

OPPOSITE: Dhritarashtra, Heavenly King of the east, surrounds himself with musicians. In some traditions, his music can convert people to Buddhism; in others, he plays so that he cannot hear and reflect dangerous sounds.

Dhritarashtra is associated with the east and has a retinue of Gandharvas (nature-spirits). He has the power to turn any sound he hears back upon its source, which can be dangerous for those around him. To prevent this, he wears a helmet that covers his ears and plays a musical instrument. He is known as the 'Upholder of the Nation'.

Virupaksa is associated with the west and has a retinue of Nagas. He protects those who practise Dharma from forces that might disrupt or impede them and avoids looking at mortals as his gaze can cause harm. It is said that in a previous life Virupaksa and Vaisravana were Garudas, great birds that prey upon snakes. When they attacked two Nagas they spotted, the Nagas proved invulnerable. They explained that they were protected by their devotion to Buddha, which convinced the birds to revere him too. All four prayed to be able to help Buddha, and were reborn in his time in order to do so.

Virudhaka is associated with the south and rules over a retinue of Kumbhandas. He causes growth of many kinds, including an increase in compassion among mortals. Like the other kings, he protects the Dharma and stands ready to repel an incursion by the Asuras. In this and all other matters, the Four Heavenly Kings answer to Sakra, who dwells in the world above theirs.

Some divine beings are referred to as Devaputtas, which essentially means they are 'young' (by Deva standards) or newly

RIGHT: Virupaksa, Heavenly King of the west, is so powerful that his gaze that can harm mortals. Like his fellows, he is considerate about his powers and avoids looking directly at anyone.

OPPOSITE: Virudhaka, Heavenly King of the south, is often depicted armed with a sword or spear. He is a fearsome defender of the Dharma, and may manifest with other Devas to protect it.

arisen into their role. Among these is Suriya, a Devaputta associated with the sun. He was once grabbed by the Asura Rahu, but was saved when the Buddha asked Rahu to let him go.

Another Devaputta is Candima, who lives in the moon. In one of the Jataka tales, the image of a hare was imprinted on the moon by Sakra in honour of the Bodhisattva's incarnation in that form. Bodhisattva was a very pious hare, and reminded his friends – a jackal, a monkey and an otter – of the importance of charity towards those less fortunate. The god Sakra decided to test them and appeared in the form

The Four Heavenly Kings in Chinese and Japanese Buddhism

The Four Heavenly Kings are, like many aspects of Buddhism, known by different names in other regions. In Japan, they are known as Tamonsr-ten, Jikoku-ten, Komoku-ten and Zojo-ten.

南方增长天王
Virudhaka in the South

of a hungry Brahmin. The three friends gave away their food, but the hare had nothing but grass. The Brahmin could not eat that, so the hare told him to build a fire. When it was hot enough the hare jumped into the flames, offering himself as a meal. Impressed, Sakra saved the hare from immolation and placed his image in the sky as a reward for his courageous self-sacrifice.

The Trāyastriṃa Devas

The Trāyastriṃa heaven lies at the summit of Mount Meru. It is the realm of the god Sakra. He is considered to be the king of all the Devas, though there are many whose nature places them beyond rulership. For example, those that exist in formless meditation, having no contact with the lower worlds, cannot be commanded. Some sources conflate Sakra and Indra, whereas others consider them to be separate gods.

Sakra is married to Suja, daughter of Vemacitrin, who is the leader of the Asuras. The Asuras intermittently but generally ineffectively make war upon the Devas, creating what amounts to a series of divine diplomatic crises. Sakra generally manages to restore peace without much violence.

The Indian god Brahma is also important in Buddhism, though he is not revered as the creator of the universe, which is the case in Hinduism. He rules the worlds known as the Brahma-Lokas, which can be reached by devout meditation. On some occasions, any Deva who dwells in these worlds is referred to as Brahma, with the ruling deity known as Brahma Shampati or Maha-Brahma. Essentially, this translates to 'great Brahma' or much more loosely to 'greatest of all the inhabitants of the Brahma worlds'. Brahma is a protector of Buddhism; he visited Buddhas on earth several times. It was he who requested that Buddha teach others, upon his attainment of enlightenment, and notably Maha-Brahma was willing to receive those teachings. This indicates that Devas are not superior to Buddhas.

OPPOSITE: The Indian god Sakra is often identified with the Jade Emperor of Chinese mythology. He is a protector of humans who vanquished evil to make the world a better place to live.

Among the other deities mentioned in Buddhist canon is Varuna, a king among the Devas, whose banner dispels fear in those who gaze upon it. Varuna is instrumental in the fight against the Asuras. Prithvi, the earth-mother, is another protector of Buddhism. One of the most iconic images of the Buddha makes reference to her, with the Buddha's hand touching the ground. This refers to an incident when the god Mara challenged Buddha's right to enlightenment. He touched the ground, and Prithvi immediately bore witness to his suitability.

The deities dwelling in this realm are often referred to as 'the thirty-three', after a Hindu tradition that there were thirty-three Devas. This number was greatly increased later, but remains symbolic as a figure of speech. Some of these 'inherited' deities play a role in the teachings or canon of Buddhism but they are all subordinate to the Buddhas in cosmic importance.

In addition, there are other Devas dwelling in the Trāyastriṃa heaven who are not numbered among the traditional thirty-three. These include Prajapati, mother of Siddhartha Gautama. She died seven days after his birth and was reborn in the Trāyastriṃa heaven as a Deva. Buddha visited her there and taught her the Dharma.

Brahma and Brahmins

It is easy to confuse the word 'Brahmin', which refers to the priestly caste, with Brahma. 'Brahma' has multiple meanings in Buddhism. It is likely this came about as a result of the Buddha using the religious terminology of his time in order to be easily understood. Brahma essentially means 'best' or 'highest', and is therefore used to indicate the importance of a particular concept, place or being.

Other Devas

Above the Tavatimsa heaven is Yama-loka. The Devas who dwell here are known as Yama Devas. Yama is also the name of the god of death, who judges those brought before him. His questioning of the dead focuses on indicators or warnings – among them old age, illness and earthly punishment of crime. Those who have not seen the warnings or failed to take note of them are sent to the hells in their next life. Some sources speak of two or even four Yamas, and some state that Yama's abode is in Naraka-loka, the hells.

Yama and Samsara

Although not responsible for causing the cycle of samsara, Yama is important to it. He governs the rebirths of humans and Devas. The only way to escape his rule is to achieve enlightenment.

BELOW: **Yama, god of death, depicted holding the wheel of life. Death and reincarnation are part of a cycle, making Yama a facilitator of rebirth rather than a grim lord of the dead.**

The Twenty-Four Devas

In Chinese Buddhism, twenty-four Devas are recognized as protectors of the Dharma. Most are gods, but numbered among them are some Naga kings and beings originating in Taoist belief. The majority of the Twenty-Four Devas (or Twenty-Four Protective Deities) come from Hinduism.

Some of the Devas are difficult to place in the cosmos as they fulfil different roles or have different identities in the various traditions. Among these is Vajrasattva. In some tradition, he is considered to be the Adi-Buddha, leader of the five Dhyani-Buddhas, and he is sometimes identified with Vajradhara. In Japanese Buddhism, Vajrasattva is known as Kongosatta.

The demon/god Mara is extremely important to the Buddhist canon as an antagonist. He constantly tries to distract people from doing right or following the Dharma, and personifies negative personality traits. The word 'Mara' can be the name of this deity but can also be a figure of speech referring to associated concepts, such as the way all beings are trapped in the endless cycle of death and rebirth. Like other Devas, Mara is not a constant being. Upon the death of one Mara, the next takes his place; a person with a great deal of accumulated bad Karma is reborn as the ultimate enemy of enlightenment. His enmity springs mainly from fear that if everyone achieves enlightenment then he will no longer have power over anyone.

Numerous stories in Buddhist canon tell of Mara's attempts to derail the activities of Buddha and his followers. Some of these are serious and rather nasty, while others are ineffectual to the point of being amusing. Most notably, Mara tried to prevent Buddha's attainment of enlightenment. He tried to win over the Buddha with desire for earthly possessions and pleasures, but he had possessed those already and given them up. After trying to appeal falsely to a sense of duty, suggesting Buddha was neglecting his responsibilities as a prince, Mara resorted to brute force. His army of demons proved ineffectual and the earth goddess sent a flood to wash them away. A subsequent effort by Mara's daughters to seduce the Buddha also failed. Finally, he tried to undermine the Buddha by saying his work was pointless if no one knew about it, but this was shot down by the earth goddess who bore witness.

ABOVE: Mara's army of demons tried their hardest to injure or at least distract the Buddha from his meditation, but ultimately they just tired themselves out.

After this, Mara ceased trying to destroy the Buddha, but did harass his followers and tried to prevent the teaching of the Dharma. As a result, he has become a metaphor for all the things that might get in the way of progress towards enlightenment, such as cravings for worldly things or negative emotions, such as pride and jealousy.

Semi-divine Beings

The Asuras are generally considered to be semi-divine They are sometimes called Danavas due to their descent from their demonic mother Danu. They are certainly much more powerful than mortals, but less so than the Devas.

The Asuras have a realm of their own, which is sometimes considered alongside the realm of the Devas and the realm of mortals as a 'good' place. On other occasions it is a 'bad' place, along with the realm of the hungry ghosts, the realm of animals and the hell realm. In one of the Jataka tales, it is revealed that once the Asuras inhabited the same realm as the Devas. They were more given to indulging in pleasures than the Devas, and ended up behaving like loutish drunks. Tiring of this, Sakra ordered they be – literally – thrown out of heaven. After tumbling down the side of Mount Meru, the Asuras realized what they had lost and were determined to regain their place. They have not managed this, and have a realm of their own.

However, although they have a native realm, Asuras can be encountered elsewhere. Often, but not always, they cause trouble. Male Asuras are renowned for being ugly and violent, while female Asuras are beautiful but ill-intentioned. They will often stir up trouble by indirect means, distracting people from good deeds and leading them into negative emotions, such as jealousy and hatred.

Asuras do not lack for ambition. Each wants to be in charge and will not tolerate someone else giving them orders. This inhibits their ability to make war on the Devas. In addition, the Devas are more powerful and better focused so tend to be victorious in open combat. Thus, the Asuras are referred to as 'laden with blessings, lacking power'.

Among the notable Asuras is Rahu, an extremely powerful being standing some 4,800 leagues (over 26,000 km) tall. He stands in the path of the Devaputta of the moon (Candima) and the Devaputta of the sun (Suriya) with his mouth open and tries to eat them, which causes eclipses. He is also one of five causes of a lack of rainfall, gathering up water in his hands and putting it in the oceans. Rahu is not all bad; eventually he went to visit the Buddha and asked to be taught about the Dharma.

Another Asura leader is Vemacitrin. During one of the many forays against the Devas, he was captured and brought before Sakra. Not deficient in courage, Vemacitrin unleashed a

BELOW: The Asuras make periodic attempts to force their way back into heaven but are inevitably driven back by the more organized and focused Devas.

OPPOSITE: Rahu is generally depicted as a serpent or dragon, usually riding in a chariot drawn by eight black horses. He is determined to eat the sun and the moon, and is the cause of eclipses.

torrent of verbal abuse on his captor, who listened patiently. When the Asura finally wound down, Sakra told him that his patience was a sign of his strength.

Sakra and Vemacitrin met under somewhat less acrimonious circumstances on another occasion, competing to see who could compose the best verse on the spot. An audience of Devas and Asuras ultimately decided to give the victory to Sakra's uplifting, educational compositions, which promoted harmony, rather than the more violent and belligerent verse of Vemacitrin. Sakra courted Vemacitrin's daughter Suja and married her after several lifetimes.

Numerous other semi-divine beings exist. Most dwell in the realm of the Four Heavenly Kings and are ruled by them. Being reborn as one of these creatures usually results from pious actions taken for the wrong reasons. Someone who does a great deal of good in the world in the hope of being rewarded with enlightenment is acting for personal gain, which is less worthy than someone doing good for the sake of others. The latter might be reborn in a higher realm, but piety out of self-interest is more likely to result in an incarnation as a being of the lower slopes of Mount Meru.

Among these beings are the Kumbhandas. These are generally similar to gnomes or fairies in other mythologies. They are associated with the south and have huge bellies and genitals. The Gandharvas can be thought of as nature-spirits. They are skilled musicians who sometimes fulfil other roles for the Devas. Sakra's charioteer is a Gandharva, while Pancasikha is the messenger of the Four Heavenly Kings. Gandharvas sometimes work alongside the Kinnaras, celestial musicians who play for the gods. Kinnaras are either half-human/half-horse, or half-human/half-bird.

Nagas are 'serpent people'. They are sometimes depicted as having the upper body of a human and the lower half of a snake, or as a multi-headed cobra. The Naga king Muchalinda used his hood to shelter Buddha for seven days while he was meditating, but other Nagas are more troublesome. Similarly, Yaksas are generally benevolent but individuals differ considerably. They are magical creatures who can change their form and are associated with nature. Female Yakshas are called Yakshini.

The Garudas, or Suparnas, are huge birds that prey on Nagas. References vary as to their exact size, but it is implied that their wingspan is measured in kilometres. They can create powerful and damaging winds by flapping their wings. Some can change into human form when it pleases them. The Garudas were charged, along with other semi-divine creatures, with the protection of Mount Meru from the Asuras. Their enmity with the Nagas is a potential problem since they share the same realm, but Buddha is known to have brought about at least a temporary cessation of hostilities.

BELOW: The Naga king Muchalinda shelters a meditating Buddha with his cobra-like hoods. Nagas seem to be as varied as humans in their motivations and personality, and can be good friends or dangerous enemies.

Other semi-divine beings or minor Devas live in the same world but are not part of the retinue of the Four Heavenly Kings. These include the Khiddapadosika, who are rather degenerate as Devas go. They are so obsessed with sensual lusts that they forget to eat or drink, bringing about their death and rebirth elsewhere. Similarly, the Manopadosika are consumed with envy, and spend so much effort on trying to satisfy this craving that their minds and bodies weaken to the point where they die.

Other beings dwelling in this world include the Sitavalahaka, who cause cool weather, and the Unhavalahaka, who cause the weather to be warm.

Among the divine or semi-divine beings who protect the Dharma are the Mahoraga. They are similar in some ways to Nagas, and may have human bodies with snake heads or snake bodies with a human-like head. They are generally stated to be huge, living within the earth, and can cause earthquakes with their movements. To be reborn as a Mahoraga, a person must live a generally good life and practise generosity but be prone to anger.

Semi-divine or supernatural beings inhabit parts of the mortal world. Among them are Rakshasas, also known as *luocha* in China and *rasetsu* in Japan. The great Indian epic *Mahabharata* tells the tale of Ravana as the enemy of Prince Rama, and portrays Rakshasas as fearsome demonic beings. They are said to inhabit the island of Sri Lanka and are sometimes considered to be Asuras. Rakshasas are sometimes portrayed as enemies of Buddhism, but sometimes they are receptive to its teachings. On one occasion, for instance, a powerful Rakshasa king named Ravana invited the Buddha to Sri Lanka to preach.

It is possible to encounter various forms of ghost in the earthly world. Some of these are termed Bhuta. They are the faintly visible shell of a recently deceased person. Invisible ghosts sometimes fly about in a particular location, usually as a result of tragic circumstances. It seems that people who do not possess the correct Yogic powers cannot perceive these unhappy spirits at all.

HUMANS VARY CONSIDERABLY THROUGHOUT A CYCLE OF THE UNIVERSE. AT TIMES, THEY ARE SMALL AND LIVE ONLY A FEW YEARS WHILE AT THE BEST TIMES OF THE CYCLE THEY ARE MUCH LARGER AND LIVE FOR TENS OF THOUSANDS OF YEARS.

Other Beings

Humans vary considerably throughout a cycle of the universe. At times, they are small and live only a few years while during the best times of the cycle they are much larger and live for tens of thousands of years. Indeed, at the beginning of a cycle, humans are not recognizable as their current form. They are formless, happy beings who float about the universe investigating its emerging wonders. Gradually, they develop physical characteristics and cravings until eventually they become what we would today perceive as a human. Thus, even the shape and form of human beings is impermanent.

Some humans transcend what mortals are normally capable of. Obviously these individuals include Buddhas and their followers who have achieved enlightenment. It is also possible to develop great psychic powers by becoming an ascetic and enduring terrible self-deprivation. The greatest of these are known in Indian mythology as Rishis, or sages. Gautama Buddha acknowledged that this path does not lead to enlightenment, but it can result in supernatural powers.

Moggallana, close disciple of the Buddha, is said to have perfected the great Yogic powers. Buddhist canon lists his powers, beginning with what today we would call telepathy. An ascetic with this ability could penetrate the minds of others and discern their thoughts. Moggallana once used this power to determine which of the Buddha's followers was corrupt, and on another occasion encountered another monk with similar abilities. After Moggallana had psychically determined that every one of the five hundred monks present was pure and saintly, one of them realized what had happened and praised him for his great power. Moggallana was also able to contact another wise monk and ask him to explain the mighty concepts he was meditating upon.

BELOW: Here, Buddha is flanked by his two chief disciples, Moggallana and Sariputta. Moggallana possessed immense Yogic powers whereas Sariputta's talent lay in his deep wisdom.

Another power that Moggallana possessed is what can be called clairaudience, the 'Divine Ear', or ability to hear what is happening in a distant place. By this means, Moggallana was able to receive the teachings of the Buddha despite being far away. The 'Divine Ear' also allows a person to hear supernatural creatures such as spirits and Devas. This talent is similar to the 'Divine Eye', which might today be called clairvoyance. It allows sight of a distant place, and of things unseen by mortals. On one occasion, Moggallana saw a Yaksha hit his friend Sariputta over the head. Sariputta felt the blow as a twinge of headache but could not see the Yaksha. On another occasion Moggallana was witness to a battle fought far off. The greatest use of this power, however, was to be able to see Karma at work in the world. Where others could only recognize the cause and effect of actions, a possessor of the 'Divine Eye' could witness them first-hand.

Another power possessed by some ascetics is teleportation or astral travel. This permits the ascetic to move into the celestial realms. Moggallana is said to have visited the realms of the Devas to teach them, and to keep in touch with the Buddha while he was there. He was able to visit a recently deceased monk in the heavenly realm and advise him on how to proceed towards nirvana.

Some ascetics also displayed what might be termed telekinesis. They were able to use their supernatural powers to move objects – including their own bodies – without touching them. This translates to the ability to fly unassisted, or to hover above the ground while meditating. Moggallana used this power to remind distracted monks – and later the god Sakra – not to become too wrapped up in their perceptions of the material world. He did so by shaking large buildings with a poke of his big toe.

ABOVE: Buddha is often depicted levitating in a lotus position. Even as a young child he displayed this ability, demonstrating his future greatness to all who observed him.

These powers are ascribed to many ascetics and sages in Indian mythology, some of whom were Bodhisattvas. The Buddha generally approved of their use for positive purposes. It was acceptable to psychically see someone in trouble far off and fly over to help them, or to fetch medicines for a friend. However, he disapproved of using powers for the sake of convenience or where it would harm living things – even insects and worms – or to show off and impress lay people. This is entirely in keeping with the general philosophy of quietly taking positive actions, however big or small.

6

NOTABLE FIGURES

A great many notable figures are associated with the life of the Buddha or the Bodhisattvas. Some of these are rulers who assisted in the spread of Buddhism while others are religious figures or important followers of the Buddha. In many cases, people closely involved with the Buddha's life are associated with figures from previous incarnations.

One of the most influential figures in the life of Buddha was his charioteer, Chandaka. Chandaka was clearly a very brave man, both morally and physically. He chose to obey the request of Siddhartha Gautama to visit the outside world, despite the edicts of the king, and reported boldly when the trips produced exactly the results that King Suddhodana had feared. When Siddhartha finally decided to leave the palace, it was Chandaka who took his personal effects home. His courage in facing the king with the

OPPOSITE: Moggallana and Sariputta leave the luxuries of their youth behind, choosing instead a simple life as disciples of the Buddha.

ABOVE: Chandaka runs behind, holding the tail of young Siddhartha Gautama's horse. Chandaka served well and bravely, eventually going forth to join his master in the Sangha.

unpleasant news of his son's departure is remarkable, and it is to Suddhodana's credit that he did not punish Chandaka for his involvement.

Chandaka became a disciple of the Buddha but was a rather toxic one. His constant insults and rudeness towards the other monks eventually resulted in censure at the First Council. Chandaka was sentenced to complete isolation and shunned by the Sangha. This – ironically or deliberately – permitted him to achieve enlightenment.

The First Disciples

After attaining enlightenment, Buddha decided to share his wonderful discovery with others. Initially, he planned to find his old teachers but they had died. Instead, he located the five ascetics he had travelled with before realizing he was on the wrong path. The five ascetics felt that Buddha had lost his way, and initially chose to ignore him. However, they were wise enough to discern that they were in the presence of someone very special and listened to his words. This was the moment where Buddha 'set the wheel of the Dharma in motion': the very first occasion upon which he shared his wisdom. The decision to become a disciple of the Buddha was a morally courageous one. It is difficult enough for anyone to admit they are wrong, but for an ascetic who has been torturing himself with self-denial for years it must have been particularly hard. The ascetics were also forced to admit that rather than being important religious figures, they were simply students who had a lot to learn. Their wisdom was sufficient, or their commitment to enlightenment pure enough, that they put aside their preconceptions and all the years sunk into austerities and embraced the 'middle way' of the Buddha.

The first of the five to understand Buddha's teachings was Kondanna, who had encountered Bodhisattva in several previous lifetimes. He was for a time one of the foremost monks of the Sangha, but after it grew to five hundred strong and began attracting huge crowds seeking wisdom, Kondanna chose to leave. He sought solitude in the Himalayas, where he could meditate in peace, and returned only to say his goodbyes before he died.

Of the five, Bhaddiya, Kondanna and Vappa embraced the Buddha's teachings most quickly, and went begging for alms while the Buddha further tutored Mahanama and Assaji. The latter was the last of the five to understand what he was being taught, but he was instrumental in converting two wise men named Upatissa and Kolita. They were religious leaders in their own right, both seeking enlightenment. When they heard of the Buddha's wisdom from Assaji, they asked to become students and were given the names Sariputta and Moggallana respectively. They became chief among the disciples of the Buddha.

Soon after the five ascetics began to follow the Buddha, a young man named Yashas (or Yasa in Pali) was also converted. He was a wealthy man, son of a merchant, but was dissatisfied

BELOW: A Vietnamese representation of the occasion Buddha 'set the wheel of Dharma in motion' by preaching his first sermon to the five ascetics who had been his companions.

ABOVE: Thai representations of Buddha, Moggallana and Sariputta. The latter were important religious figures in their own right before they met Buddha and became his disciples.

with his life as it was. Although not ordained as a monk, Yashas became a lay disciple. He was followed by his wife and family and then their friends. Ultimately, Yashas brought with him around fifty new converts. This was the beginning of a religious community that would grown to be hundreds or thousands strong.

Sariputta and Moggallana

The man who would become known as Moggallana was originally named Kolita. He was born into a wealthy and powerful Brahmin family descended from Rishi Mudgala, one of the ancient sages. Upatissa, who would become Sariputta, was born on the same day. The boys grew up together and were great friends, though they had very different personalities. Where Upatissa was bold and sought adventure, Kolita was more concerned with protecting and nurturing what he already had.

Eventually, their youthful play became less satisfactory. Both expected to enjoy the Hill Festival held annually at the capital, but despite having good places reserved from where they could observe and join in the festivities, both were disappointed. The first day had pleased them but the second felt strangely flat, and neither slept well that night. As the third day of the festival began, both agreed that they wanted something more from life than empty and fleeting amusement.

Although each had come to the conclusion independently, both friends realized they sought the same things – enlightenment and a release from the cycle of pointless suffering and stale amusement. They set off to become ascetics and learn wisdom, hoping to find a teacher who could impart unto them what they sought. That teacher would be Siddhartha Gautama, but at that point he was around sixteen years old. Thus, as the future Buddha was celebrating his marriage, his future foremost disciples were setting out on the journey that would lead them to him.

Kolita and Upatissa sought out many teachers. Some had wisdom and some were on a false path, but none could offer what they needed until they met Sanjaya. There is no record of exactly what he taught them, but they were certainly impressed enough to become close followers. It seems that Sanjaya would not deal in absolutes and answers, but quite the opposite. He acknowledged that some things are not knowable to mortals and some questions cannot be answered. It is therefore necessary to remain impartial and to observe the cosmos from a detached viewpoint.

HE ACKNOWLEDGED THAT SOME THINGS ARE NOT KNOWABLE TO MORTALS AND SOME QUESTIONS CANNOT BE ANSWERED. IT IS THEREFORE NECESSARY TO REMAIN IMPARTIAL AND TO OBSERVE THE COSMOS FROM A DETACHED VIEWPOINT.

Sanjaya's stance was interesting but it did not provide what Kolita and Upatissa were looking for. While Sanjaya thought it was not possible to know if there was another world beyond that perceived by mortals, the friends were inclined to believe one existed. Sanjaya candidly admitted that they had learned everything that they could from him, so Kolita and Upatissa moved on.

Their time with Sanjaya was not wasted. While they had not been given any answers, Kolita and Upatissa had been trained how to analyse and meditate upon the teachings of others, and applied these skills to what they were told by the teachers they met. In all cases, they could poke holes in the teachings of others and at the same time present a coherent argument that could not be refuted in defence of their own beliefs. One after another, philosophers and mystics failed to withstand their questioning.

After nearly two decades of wandering, Kolita and Upatissa returned to their homeland of Magadha. They decided to split up and cover more ground – physically as well as spiritually – on the understanding that whichever found a true teacher first would bring word to the other. At this time, Buddha had established his Sangha and missionaries were setting out to teach wherever their wanderings took them.

Upatissa encountered a monk named Assaji, one of Buddha's very first disciples, and immediately acknowledged his worth. Upon request, Assaji presented a simple overview of the Buddha's teachings and, despite his keen insight, Upatissa could find nothing wrong with it. Assaji then recited a stanza that made Upatissa realize he had found the teacher he was looking for.

ABOVE: Upon joining the Sangha, the man named Upatissa received a new identity as Sariputta. Having heard the Buddha teach, he went on to achieve enlightenment without further assistance.

Kolita had the same reaction when he heard the stanza repeated. Both wanted to go to meet Buddha immediately, but decided to inform Sanjaya of their discovery. This would give him the chance to pursue enlightenment instead of his own worthy but flawed philosophy. Sanjaya decided not to go to the Buddha, and attempted to persuade his former students to stay with him as co-leaders of their community. They opted not to accept this great honour and left Sanjaya, who decided he preferred to be the leader of his own group rather than a student in a better one. To Sanjaya's great dismay, about half of his five hundred disciples followed Upatissa and Kolita.

Buddha was teaching when Upatissa and Kolita arrived, and instantly perceived that they would be the greatest of his disciples. He ordained them on the spot and renamed Kolita as Maha-Moggallana, 'great one of the Moggallana clan'. Upatissa was remained 'son of Sari' – Sariputta – after his mother. The two retired to meditate while Buddha began teaching the two hundred and fifty former students of Sanjaya they had brought with them.

Sariputta meditated in a nearby cave, visiting the town to hear Buddha speak and to obtain alms. In fourteen days of powerful meditation, he achieved Arahant status. Moggallana, on the other hand, had more of a struggle. One problem he faced was that his body kept trying to fall asleep while he meditated. Buddha was aware of his struggle, and taught him ways to overcome his drowsiness. It was still difficult, but that was part of the process. By conquering his body's disobedient need for sleep, Moggallana could train himself to focus more closely on the teachings.

Eventually, Moggallana managed to conquer his drowsiness, which was a manifestation of the third of five hindrances. The first two, desire and ill-will, had long ago been defeated during his time as an ascetic. Once sloth was defeated, Moggallana learned to suppress restlessness and worry, and finally doubt, all with the help of the Buddha. This enabled him to enter the meditative state known as *jhana*. The process was not perfect at once; when Moggallana became distracted by worldly thoughts the Buddha offered more guidance, until he was able to enter the meditative state reliably and stay there. From there, Moggallana learned to attain the higher *jhanas* until, after seven rather intense days, he attained enlightenment.

Moggallana and Sariputta became the foremost among the disciples of Buddha, with Ananda as his attendant. This pattern was repeated with all Buddhas; each had an attendant and two main disciples, who were often reincarnations of previous disciples. Buddha described the arrangement as being similar to the chief ministers of a kingdom. Ananda, with his perfect memory, acted as a sort of treasurer of knowledge. The chief disciples had responsibilities according to their character; Sariputta was his general and Moggallana the minister for internal affairs. Later in life, Buddha relied upon these three to speak and teach for him when he became tired. Others might go far abroad in the world to teach the Buddha's wisdom, but only these three taught in his presence.

The appointment of Sariputta and Moggallana as chief disciples did not sit well with all of the other Sangha members. Many thought that the first five ascetics should be their leaders, or other notables who had been with the Buddha for longer than Sariputta and Moggallana. Buddha told them that the two had been with him for many

Different Paths to Enlightenment

It is notable that Moggallana and Sariputta were very different as saints, just as Kolita and Upatissa were as boys. Moggallana took a short and difficult route to enlightenment with the help of Buddha, while Sariputta's method was slower but easier. He is considered superior since he did not require assistance; hearing the teachings and thinking about them was enough. Moggallana focused more on the liberation of the mind and development of supernatural powers where Sariputta emphasized wisdom. While both were highly capable in all areas, their differing focus made them an effective team in leading the other members of the Sangha. Buddha, of course, combined both aspects in a single, perfect whole.

lifetimes, working towards their present status through their various incarnations.

Moggallana and Sariputta had known one another in thirty lives, and had met Bodhisattva in each of them. Moggallana knew Bodhisattva in one more life, during which Moggallana was incarnated as the god Sakra. In some of these lives, Moggallana and Sariputta were friends of Bodhisattva, in some his brothers, sons or loyal associates. When Bodhisattva was incarnated as Sakra, Moggallana was the sun god and Sariputta was the moon. In one incarnation, Sariputta was king of the Nagas and Moggallana was his enemy, the king of the Supannas.

Sariputta died a few months before Buddha, and soon afterwards the evil god Mara tried to take Moggallana by entering his body through the bowels. Moggallana recognized the intrusion and ordered the god out of his body. Mara was amazed that anyone, even Buddha, could discern him so quickly, but Moggallana knew him from many previous incarnations. Most people cannot recall their previous lives but this was one of Moggallana's great psychic powers.

BELOW: Sariputta died peacefully in the house where he was born, surrounded by monks from the Sangha. His friend Moggallana met a rather more brutal end.

Moggallana died soon after his great friend Sariputta. As with most aspects of their lives, the circumstances of their deaths were quite different. Sariputta was at his parental home, peaceful and surrounded by monks. Moggallana, on the other hand, died violently. The leader of the Jain religion, Nathaputta, had died. The leaderless Jains were in turmoil; their adherents were leaving to seek wisdom elsewhere. Meanwhile, Moggallana was a prominent figure who was attracting followers from all quarters.

Some of the worst of the Jains decided they should do away with Moggallana, but did not want to get their hands dirty. They hired a band of criminals to murder him. Ironically, Moggallana felt his work was done and was ready to give up his mortal existence. The Jains could simply have waited for him to die. Instead,

LEFT: Moggallana was not quite perfect, and was unable to prevent his enemies from murdering him. It was an empty victory however; he had achieved everything he needed to and was ready to enter nirvana.

their hirelings went to the remote forest hut where Moggallana was living in solitude, intent on a killing. While he was ready to leave the mortal world, Moggallana did not permit the murderers to find him. He used his supernatural abilities to vanish before the criminals arrived, and repeated the trick each day when they came back. In so doing, he showed a sort of mercy the criminals would be unlikely to understand. Avoiding them was not about saving his own life but rather protecting them from the karmic consequences of murdering such a holy man.

However, the criminals were persistent and on the seventh day Moggallana was unable to repeat his previous feats. This was due to an old misdeed that had never been made right. The criminals caught Moggallana and laid about him, beating him savagely and breaking his limbs. They left him for dead and went to claim their payment.

Moggallana was not yet quite ready to leave the world. He used his great psychic strength to support his body on one last journey to see the Buddha. Once he had arrived, he died. The piece of negative Karma that prevented his escape from the

ABOVE: A fifteenth-century depiction of Buddha teaching King Bimbisara, who was a good friend to the Sangha. This proved his undoing, when he became ensnared in the fiendish plots of the nefarious Devadatta.

murderers did not affect his entry into nirvana since it was of his mortal life only and he had already achieved detachment from all things worldly.

The Buddha was not sad at the deaths of his most worthy disciples, though he noted that the Sangha was diminished in their absence. Their lives had been a marvellous thing and inspiring to all who heard of them, while their deaths were inevitable and of little consequence since they were freed of the cycle of samsara.

King Ajatasattu

King Ajatasattu was the son of King Bimbisara of Magadha, whose realm lay in eastern India. He founded the city of Pataliputra, where modern-day Patna stands. As a warrior king, he conquered Kosala and other neighbouring areas, establishing one of the most powerful kingdoms of his time. Ajatasattu was the sponsor of the First Council, though he was not initially a friend to the Sangha. Indeed, he was a central figure in one of the greatest tests the Buddha ever faced. Ajatasattu was always destined to be the enemy of his father. While she was pregnant, King Bimbisara's wife desired to drink some of his blood, and the king gladly offered her some. When they learned of this, the king's religious advisors warned that the child would be his undoing. His wife tried to abort the baby several times, but he asked her to desist. She agreed, but plotted to kill the child when it was born.

In the event, the child was taken away to a place of safety and eventually his mother came to love and accept him. He was raised as a prince and well treated by King Bimbisara, despite the warnings about his destiny. In time, Ajatasattu would have ascended to the throne as a well-respected ruler. However, he was impatient.

At that time, the Sanga surrounding the Buddha was flourishing. Many of the monks had become Arahants, but Devadatta was among those who had not. Indeed, he struggled with the path to enlightenment and instead focused on developing his own power – both mystical and political. Devadatta went to Prince Ajatasattu as a missionary and easily won him over with a demonstration of his psychic powers. The prince bestowed lavish gifts upon the Sangha, which fed Devadatta's ego and ambition. He suggested that the Buddha should retire and turn over leadership to Devadatta. Buddha disagreed, pronouncing him unworthy.

This was certainly true, but Devadatta did not want to hear it. Recognizing that Prince Ajatasattu's ruthless ambition matched his own, Devadatta set about manipulating him into deposing his father. He proposed a deal whereby Ajatasattu took over the kingdom and Devadatta seized control of the Sangha.

BELOW: A depiction of King Ajatasattu and his wife, at the Kizil Caves in Xinjiang, China. This image was created around 600–650 CE.

MEANWHILE DEVADATTA HAD FAILED TO MURDER THE BUDDHA AND TAKE OVER THE WHOLE SANGHA SO HE INSTEAD LED AN INSURRECTION. SOME OF THE MONKS THOUGHT THE LIFESTYLE OF THE SANGHA WAS A BIT SOFT, AND WANTED MORE SEVERE AUSTERITIES TO BE THE NORM.

Ajatasattu agreed, and sent one or more assassins – sources vary on the exact number – to slay the Buddha. Others were sent to kill the assassins, and yet more to kill them in turn, so that the trail would not lead back to Ajatasattu. The assassins were overcome by the Buddha's holiness and instead joined the Sangha. Devadatta made more attempts, throwing rocks and sending a maddened elephant, but he was ultimately powerless against the Buddha.

Meanwhile, Ajatasattu attempted to carry out his own part of the plan. He was caught approaching the king with a knife, but rather than punish him, King Bimbisara chose to give him the throne. This satisfied Ajatasattu but Devadatta was less impressed. The old king was still a friend to the Buddha and might be an obstacle to his own ambitions. He urged Ajatasattu to do away with his father, so Bimbisara was imprisoned with the intent of starving him to death. His loyal wife sneaked him food, which frustrated Ajatasattu sufficiently that he ordered the former king murdered.

Meanwhile Devadatta had failed to murder the Buddha and take over the whole Sangha so he instead led an insurrection. Some of the monks thought the lifestyle of the Sangha was a bit soft and wanted more severe austerities to be the norm. Devadatta appealed to this sentiment, and ultimately led five hundred of the monks astray. This was a crisis for the Buddha and a real test of his leadership. Opinions were divided about whose way was best: the strict rules of Devadatta or the middle way espoused by Buddha. His solution was typically understated yet effective. He sent Sariputta and Moggallana, his chief disciples, to the breakaway Sangha.

Thinking they were defecting, Devadatta made an address to his followers, then went to sleep. Sariputta and Moggallana then spoke to the wayward monks and won them over with reasoned thinking and calm wisdom.

As to Ajatasattu, he came to regret his actions. This was not the first life in which he had been at odds with his father, nor was it the first time he had associated with those who did bad deeds. Yet he could and did change. It is said that he could not sleep without nightmares after the murder of King Bimbisara, and that he understood that the sinful begin to experience the punishments they are due before the end of their current lives.

Filled with shame, Ajatasattu could not face the Buddha for a long time. He did consult with other religious figures, but none

BELOW: The remains of the prison in which King Bimbisara was kept still exist today. The modern city of Patna lies adjacent to his ancient capital of Pataliputra.

could provide him with the absolution he needed. In the end, Ajatasattu went to see Buddha in a state of great trepidation. He was greeted politely and treated with honour, and the Buddha forgave him his sins. Some considered Ajatasattu should have been punished more harshly, but Buddha told them the king had made his own fate and would pay the price without anyone else imposing penances or punishments.

Ajatasattu no longer suffered terrifying nightmares after his absolution, though he remained an ambitious and warlike ruler. Not long before the death of Buddha, Ajatasattu sent messengers asking if he had a good prospect of victory over the Vajjians. The reply was negative; however, Buddha told Ajatasattu that once the Vajjians ceased to follow the Buddha's teachings, an attack by Ajatasattu would be victorious. This did not happen until after the Buddha had died.

Ajatasattu never visited Buddha again but was filled with love for him and fainted in horror when he heard of Buddha's death. After a period of despair and mourning, Ajatasattu created memorials to Buddha and pledged to support the Sangha to the best of his ability. This he did, famously sponsoring the First Council, which was one of the most important events in the history of Buddhism.

Ajatasattu was eventually killed by his own son, Udayabhadra, who was born on the day King Bimbisara was killed. Since he had committed parricide, one of the worst crimes possible according to Buddhist belief, he was reborn in hell, where he must suffer for sixty thousand years before being absolved of his crime. This is particularly unfortunate since had he not committed the murder he would have achieved enlightenment at his final meeting with the Buddha instead of mere forgiveness for his part in the plots to kill Buddha.

King Kalasoka

The dynasty of King Ajatasattu was characterized by sons murdering their fathers. Ajatasattu was killed by his son Udayabhadra, who ruled for sixteen years before being killed by Anuruddha. He in turn was murdered by Munda, who was slain by his son Nagadasaka. This was too much for the people of the

OPPOSITE: Emperor Ashoka was instrumental in the spread of Buddhism. It is likely he turned to the peaceful religion after sickening of the violence necessary in his campaigns of conquest.

Westward Contact

Nothing in the history of the world ever happened in isolation. Contact between the eastern parts of India and the ancient Greeks was not confined to a single epic campaign by Alexander the Great or the defeat of the satrapies his retreating armies left behind. Trade and diplomacy flowed back and forth across Persia from India to Greece and thence to Europe, and with it culture and religion.

Emperor Ashoka is known to have sponsored missionaries headed for foreign nations, so it is not beyond the bounds of possibility that official missions went westward. Even if they did not, there is evidence of cultural intercourse between India and the Mediterranean world in antiquity. Buddhism did not take hold in Europe until modern times, but it may have been known there far earlier.

BELOW: Alexander the Great's victory over King Porus in 326 BCE created Macedonian enclaves in western India. Cultural and religious interaction certainly took place.

kingdom, who drove out Nagadasaka and installed his minister Susunaga as ruler. He was succeeded peacefully by his son Kalasoka, who moved the capital to Pataliputra. Kalasoka is notable primarily for sponsoring the Second Council, a century after the death of the Buddha.

Emperor Ashoka

Ashoka, or Asoka, was the last emperor of the Mauryan Empire, which was founded in 322 BCE by Chandragupta Maurya. India was at that time heavily disrupted as a result of the campaigns of Alexander the Great. As the Macedonians retreated, a power vacuum developed, which permitted the rise of the new empire. Defeating an incursion by Alexander's successors, the Mauryan dynasty continued to grow over the decades.

With its capital at what is now Patna, the Mauryan empire came to dominate a region from the Himalayas to central India, and from modern Pakistan and Iran to Assam. It reached its peak under the rule of Ashoka, who conducted a bloody campaign of conquest and pacification in Kalinga. This was facilitated by a well-organized state and an experienced standing army, but it may be that the price paid weighed heavily on Emperor Ashoka.

Emperor Ashoka was respectful of the religions of his time but did not originally favour any of them. This changed when a novice monk named

LEFT: **Emperor Ashoka funded the construction of stupas all across India, as well as missionaries to other areas. Surviving stonework contains records of his edicts on the subject of religion.**

Nigrodha told him the story known as *Appamada-vagga*. This tale concerns heedfulness, among other virtues. The Buddha taught that those who are heedful should be considered to be alive even after their death, while those who are heedless might as well be dead.

Ashoka renounced his support for various religions and embraced Buddhism, implementing the teachings of Dharma as his state religion. He commissioned a great many works of art and public constructions, including pillars inscribed with his edicts. Those that survive contain some of the oldest writings in India. He is also credited with having eighty-four thousand pagodas or stupas built to facilitate the spread of Buddhism. While this number is subject to the usual considerations of exaggeration and dramatic effect, Ashoka certainly funnelled a huge amount of money and effort into supporting the religion.

Although Ashoka's support was greatly beneficial to the spread of Buddhism, it also made it possible for scam artists to enrich themselves by pretending to be Buddhist monks. Initially Ashoka did not fully comprehend the problem, and was annoyed by the refusal of devout monks to perform ceremonies alongside the fakers. However, Ashoka's edict that they do so was ignored,

even under direct threat of death, and he was made aware of the problem. His sponsorship of the Third Council permitted the resolution of various problems and the expulsion of unworthy monks.

The Six Non-Buddhist Teachers

During the lifetime of Gautama Buddha there were six notable teachers of opposing views. They are sometimes known as the Six Heretical Teachers. They not only contradicted the teachings of the Buddha, but also went against the accepted Brahmin doctrine of the day. Most of them contended that moral actions have no consequences, whereas the Buddhist view is that they most certainly do. The six were consulted by King Ajatasattu before he went to see the Buddha. Their answers to his questions failed to satisfy him.

ABOVE: Nigantha Nataputta, also known as Mahavir, is often credited with founding Jainism. However, it is more accurate to say that he was one of the figures who revealed its central truths.

Purana Kassapa did not believe there was a link between actions of the body and responsibility taken by the soul. In this, he rejected the very concept of morality, since there were no consequences of good or bad actions. It is said he claimed to be omniscient and that he eventually committed suicide by drowning himself. Makkhali Gosala, on the other hand, believed in fate and inevitability. Since nothing can be done to change a person's fate, they must be resigned to it. Ajita Kesakambala taught that the cosmos was built from simple elements and that people have one life. They might as well enjoy it as much as they could while it lasted, and there were no consequences of good or evil actions after death.

Pakudha Kaccayana taught that humans were made of seven basic elements – earth, wind, water, fire, suffering, pleasure and soul. All things were defined by the interactions of these

elements, making people and their choices largely irrelevant. Meanwhile, Sanjaya Belatthiputta had no definitive answers to give on any of the big questions. He taught that there might or might not be an existence after the present one. The Buddha's chief disciples studied with him for a while and suggested he become a follower of the Buddha when they learned of his wisdom. Sanjaya declined, preferring to remain a big (if ignorant) fish in a small pool than to subordinate his ego to someone who actually did have the answers.

ABOVE: A Chinese depiction of the Six Heretical Teachers. These figures attracted large numbers of followers but were ultimately eclipsed by the Buddha's disciples.

The sixth of these teachers was Nigantha Nataputta, who is generally (but incorrectly) considered to be the founder of Jainism. In many ways, the Jain faith is similar to Buddhism. Those who seek enlightenment must do so through non-violence to all living things. As with Buddhism, Jainism has multiple sources, known as Tirthankaras, who revealed the truth necessary to achieve liberation from the cycle of samsara. Nigantha Nataputta was the twenty-fourth Tirthankara. He is also known as Mahavira.

Cinca Manavika

Cinca Manavika was one of the enemies faced by the Buddha. Her actions were instigated by those who realized they stood to lose out due to the Buddha's increasing popularity. These were ascetics who expounded other faiths and teachings. They selected Cinca Manavika for her beauty, and set her the task of discrediting the Buddha.

The plan was well laid. Cinca Manavika allowed herself to be seen going to the Jetavana monastery at night carrying flowers. She slipped away once she was unobserved, but was careful to be back at the monastery early in the morning. Again, she allowed

herself to be seen returning. To a casual observer, it would be obvious that she had spent the night at the monastery. If asked, she said she had spent the night with the Buddha.

After a few months, Cinca Manavika began to pad her clothing to make it look like she was pregnant, gradually increasing the size of her bump to simulate an advancing pregnancy. After nine months, she burst in while the Buddha was teaching and confronted him, to all appearances pregnant with his child. Cinca Manavika denounced the Buddha, claiming he had impregnated her and then left her to her own devices. The Buddha calmly replied that nobody but he and she could know what had really happened.

ABOVE: Cinca Manakiva accused Buddha of impregnating her in front of the monks he was teaching. The god Sakra, a protector of Buddhism, exposed her lies with the help of Devas in the form of cloth-nibbling rats.

The god Sakra was as usual watching over the Buddha, and sent some minor Devas in the form of rats to assist with the problem. They nibbled away the strings that held Cinca Manavika's padding and the clothing that covered it, revealing her pregnancy to be a deception. This angered the assembled monks, who denounced Cinca Manavika. She fled in terror, meeting with an accidental death in the process.

The Buddha later explained to his followers that this is the nature of liars; they will do as they please no matter who it harms. He revealed that Cinca Manavika had done something similar in a previous life. When she was the consort to a king, she fell in love with his son. Rejected by the prince, she disfigured herself and claimed he had made advances that she had rejected. The prince, she claimed, had inflicted injuries upon her in his anger. The prince was banished, but when the truth came to light, Cinca Manavika's previous incarnation was severely punished

This is one of numerous morality tales to be found throughout Buddhist literature. Good deeds are ultimately rewarded and those who commit evil get their comeuppance. The cycle continues until the person changes their ways and begins to progress towards nirvana. Ultimately, this is a truth that pervades all Buddhist teachings – a being is not immutable but is the sum of its choices and experiences. Everyone is the captain of their metaphysical fate – they can suffer punishments for bad deeds or remain in the cycle of samsara forever, but they always have the choice to begin working towards nirvana.

Final Notes

Buddhist mythology is a huge subject, made more complex by the existence of multiple traditions. It is not possible to deal with all the alternate names, versions of tales and unique aspects found across the major schools in a single work of this size. Thus, the emphasis is on Theravada and Mahayana traditions, with a lesser emphasis on the Vajrayana school of Buddhism. Japanese and Chinese Buddhism arguably deserve their own treatment, which space precludes. It is to be hoped that this volume provides an overview and starting point for exploration of this vast subject, with all its wondrous stories and quiet wisdom.

BELOW: Makha Bucha Day is one of the most important festivals for Theravada Buddhists. It commemorates an early gathering of the Buddha's disciples and is held in the third lunar month of the year.

INDEX

References to illustrations are in *italics*.

PICTURE CREDITS

Alamy: 6 (CPA Media), 8 (Godong), 9 (Leslie Wilk), 11 (CPA Media), 14 (Prisma Archivo), 16 (Maciej Wojtkowiak), 18 (Chronicle), 19 (BasPhoto), 20 (Art Directors & TRIP), 21 (PrachiDamle/Stockimo), 23 (CPA Media), 25 (Artokoloro), 32 (ephotocorp), 36 (Science History Images), 41 (Godong), 47 (Album), 56 (Art Directors & TRIP), 59 (Godong), 61 (Art Directors & TRIP), 73 (Yvette Cardozo), 75 (Godong), 76 (Album), 80 (Art Collection 4), 82 (LMA/AW), 90 (Trevor Thompson), 93 (Jane Sweeney), 103 (Asar Studios), 104 (Zoonar), 105 (Matija Brumen), 107 & 111 (Robert Harding), 112/113 (Angelo Hornak), 121 (agefotostock), 125 (Melvyn Longhurst), 128 (Maciej Wojtkowiak), 129 (World Religions Photo Library), 132 (Heritage Image Partnership), 134 (Hum Historical), 136 (Gianni Muratore), 140 (Robert Harding), 142 (Godong), 154 (sherab), 165 (umedha malinda), 166 (Album), 179 (agefotostock), 181 (Paul Martin), 183 (Robert Harding), 185 (Sergi Reboredo), 188 (imageBROKER), 190 (Lebrecht Music & Arts), 193 (CPA Media), 197 (Clement Cazottes), 200 (Godong), 201 (dpa picture alliance), 202 (Larind), 209 (Interfoto), 212 (Album), 214 (Classic Stock), 215 (agefotostock)

Bridgeman Images: 115 (Sylvain Collet)

Bridgeman Images/British Library Board: 29, 87, 124, 163, 198, 206

Dreamstime: 5 (Steve Estvanik), 13 (Ugeshkumar), 31 (ePhotocorp), 33 (NGSpacetime), 43 (Haotian), 48 (Untukbikinpaypal), 60 (Steve Estvanik), 66 (Maneeshcoin), 70/71 (Cascoly), 171 (Dbajurin), 172 (Kravka), 174/175 (Devy), 184 (Klodien), 217 (Luckybai), 219 (Structuresxphotography)

Getty Images: 30 (Poorfish), 42 (Oliver Strewe), 49 (Art Media/Print Collector), 54 (M Borchi/De Agostini), 57 & 89 (G Dagli Orti/De Agostini), 95 (Reza), 168 (Philippe Lissac/Godong)

Getty Images/Heritage Images: 46, 63, 78 (CM Dixon), 97, 119 (Ashmolean Museum), 127, 144, 153, 160, 191 (Ashmolean Museum), 194, 196 (CM Dixon)

Getty Images/Universal Images Group: 45 (Werner Forman), 50 & 58 (Godong), 62 (Universal History Archive), 67 (Sepia Times), 69 & 74 (Godong)

Getty Images/Universal Images Group/Pictures From History: 85, 86, 92, 96, 108, 114 (David Henley), 177, 178, 216

Licensed under the Creative Commons Attribution 2.0 Generic Licence: 64/65, 79 & 126 all (Photo Dharma)

Licensed under the Creative Commons Attribution-Share Alike 2.5 Generic Licence: 211 (BPG)

Licensed under the Creative Commons Attribution-Share Alike 3.0 Unreported Licence: 207, 218

Licensed under the Creative Commons Attribution-Share Alike 4.0 International Licence: 186 (Nyarlathotep1001)

Los Angeles County Museum of Art: 130

Metropolitan Museum of Art, New York: 15, 26, 28, 35, 38, 52, 53, 55, 72, 83, 84, 98, 99, 100, 118/119, 122, 133, 137, 138, 139, 146-152, 156, 159, 162, 176, 208

National Museum of Asian Art, Smithsonian Institution, Washington D.C.: 143

Public Domain: 12, 170, 204

Shutterstock: 157 (Maxim Popykin)

Walters Art Museum, Baltimore: 116/117 (Gift from Doris Duke Charitable Foundation's Southeast Asian Art Collection)